DESOLATE

CAROLYN R. PARSONS

DESOLATE

CAROLYN R. PARSONS

ENGEN
BOOKS

Published in Canada by Engen Books, St. John's, NL.

Library and Archives Canada Cataloguing in Publication information is available at request.

ISBN-13: 978-1-77478-095-4

Distributed by:
Engen Books
www.engenbooks.com
submissions@engenbooks.com

First mass market paperback printing: March 2022

Cover Design: Ellen Curtis

To my children,
Alyssa,
Christie,
Ollie,
and Martina,
because the future belongs to you.

CHAPTER ONE

The hungry month. That's what the old people called March. A roaring storm and massive sea surge rolled in with a ferocious bellow on the coast of Newfoundland Island the night of the full moon. The two-day squall battered the shore and saltwater spray wrapped a briny white ribbon around the ragged trees that lined the bay. Pegged a once-in-a-hundred-years storm by meteorologists, there had been three as big as this one, just these past two months.

After it subsided, the tides gurgled with an angry energy under the ice and snow drifts and swirled across marshes and rocks.

"In like a lion, out like a lamb," locals quoted, ever hopeful, always wrong. March was consistently cold and white and long to its bitter end.

Heavy Labrador Land ice had become heavier in recent years. The changing tides, the rising seas, and frequent high winds brought it earlier and closer to the shores every season.

Those floes blocked any movement by ferry from tiny Desolate Island to the mainland, and the long, grey rent in the centre of the white expanse, left behind by the wake of the vessel, prevented any transport across by car or skidoo.

Jean Adler sighed and laid down the binoculars, happy the storm had ended, but the ice that it left behind, jam-packed tight to the shore, meant no ferry could bring freight or mail. She walked over and flicked the wall switch to turn on some light, the dawn brighter outside than the house was.

"Damn." Her voice echoed in the empty kitchen. The power often flickered and blinked and sometimes went out for days when the wind whipped and gusted around the poles, striking down power lines. Sometimes it knocked out the transformers. Usually within a short time, the hardy linesmen, once weather and ice allowed, had the place illuminated and back into mid-twenty-first century in no time flat. It was frustrating. She longed for the geothermal heating and underground electrical grid of Ontario with no poles and rare outages.

She'd gained other, more important things by moving to Newfoundland, but they were hard to remember when she craved a hot coffee and a shower and there was no power. She tapped the screen of her mobile device. The A-Tab had plenty of charge but no connection. There was no Wi-Fi due to the power outage but surely TeluBell was available?

"I guess the tower is down," she said to the dead phone. Her cat, Tom, meowed in response and she petted him and tossed the useless device on to the table.

Hauling out a drawer, she scrounged around for an ancient radio, found C-Cell batteries in the depths of a second junk drawer, and flicked the buttons to get the news the old-fashioned way.

There was nothing but static on FM. The AM dial was the same. No VOCM. No News director, Colleen Harrison, to explain and reassure, her confident voice as familiar and soothing as the crackle of the wood stove that provided the only source of heat on this strange morning.

Jean peered out the kitchen window. Smoke rose in grey puffs from next door. Across the cove three more smudges of grey floated against the red dusk. There were no yellow glows in the windows, however. This was a full-blown blackout.

Across to the east the sun rose, heaving itself over the horizon with stoic determination. The sky was an unusual colour, with a reddish-orange glow that climbed from the land and spread across and above it, rather than coming from the sky and spreading down. It had lit up the morning enough to see through the binoculars but not enough to fully illuminate the kitchen. Dread trickled down her spine and through her nervous system, lifting the hairs on her arms and the back of her neck.

Jean whipped around the AM stations again until finally a voice, muffled in the static, broke through the air waves. She cranked the volume a bit and strained to hear as the voice drifted in and out.

"What the hell?" she said after listening for a few moments. Tom jumped and her heart pummeled her chest as the words on the radio penetrated her brain. *Static static static — massive destruction — static — electronics down — static — satellites destroyed — static static static static static.*

She listened harder. Even the satellites that circled the earth and provided the vast communication connections that had made the world so much smaller were destroyed?

"No fucking way. That's FoxCan, it must be. Can't believe a word of it, Tom," she said.

The announcer's voice folded into the static-filled hiss.

In a fit of pique, Jean picked up the little radio and shook it, moving the dial back and forth, knocking it off the station altogether. Regretting her temper, she attempted to restore the connection, turning the dial back one click at a time.

The door behind her creaked, the knock that accompanied its opening a mere courtesy.

"I would have called, but there are no phones, no cell, no power, and worse, no TV stream. I went to the ferry this morning and it's not running because it isn't allowed to without communication programs, especially in this thick ice, so it's stuck over on the other side," Max Dawe said. He was her closest neighbour and her house had formerly belonged to his uncle who sold it when he moved into a nursing home.

"Everything is down, all over the world. I think."

"What? I'm doubtful that's true. Where did you hear that?"

She lifted the radio up like a trophy. "I put some batteries in the old girl since the APP doesn't work. I could only pick up one station and they're reporting something has happened that knocked out all the satellites, the power, the television, essentially all types of communications... well, everywhere. It keeps going in and out, but I think that's what it's saying."

"That's crazy. Is it to do with the war?" Max pulled off his wool cap and slid out a chair to sit.

Jean put a teacup in front of him and went to get the kettle.

"I think so. I don't know. Maybe there has been a nuclear attack, maybe a cyber-attack. Maybe a computer virus. Not sure, but this is serious for us if it's true. We're out of touch here on the island. I wonder if I should call a state of emergency." She had never had to do that before in her years as mayor.

"How do you call it, if you can't call people?" Max popped a toothpick out of the little yellow plastic barrel in the middle of the table, stuck it in his mouth and chewed. He'd quit smoking when he turned eighty and had gnawed the little wooden sticks constantly ever since.

"I don't know. I guess we go door to door and call it? But I'm not comfortable making that decision. The town hall is going to be freezing. Here, kettle's boiled, watch out, let me pour."

Max leaned back to prevent getting scalded as she covered his teabag, filling the cup. He stirred it, squeezing the bag to darken the water, contemplating its transformation to a dark amber colour. "Sounds a bit drastic, don't it, Jean maid?"

Jean poured the hot water into the French press. "Max, I'm not a person who panics but I think we have to get started with the plan. I don't think we need to implement everything, but we have to declare it and then go from there. If we find out it's not so bad, we pull back but without power and internet, what else is there to do anyway?"

"You got a point. Nobody's going to be able to do any work for A-Zon without power or internet," he said.

"Maybe first thing, Max, you could take my car, she's fully charged, drive around and get the council members here for, let's say at ten? You'll have to start her though, with the button, can't do it from the A-Zon. Meanwhile I'll grab a bite to eat and set things up. Somebody else might have heard what's on the radio, though I know nearly all use their devices for news now. Let's see what they all think. We'll take a vote on it at the meeting and go from there."

"Oh, 'tis serious if you're letting me drive your fancy car." He grinned. "Good idea, Mrs. Mayor. I'll go now, the minute I finishes me tea." Max saluted, then winked and nodded.

A short while later, tea and a biscuit demolished in record time, the door closed behind him. Jean picked up the radio, twisting the dial again, click by click until the AM station burst in, the signal stronger than before. She could tell it was a Newfoundland voice, so it was not FoxCan after all.

He repeated the information, in a loop, over and over.

Everything was shut down everywhere. Towns were encouraged to implement their emergency plans and conserve their stocks of Cleanfuel and food, lather, rinse, repeat until he faded out once more. She gave the dial a slow twist going right to the end and back but there was still only static.

"Okay," she said out loud. "Implement the emergency plan. That settles that." Jean went to her office and pulled a file from a cabinet drawer. She kept two copies of every valuable document, one on site, one off. She also had a digital copy and the computer was charged, but the printer wouldn't print without power.

The meeting would be held by the light of the March sun shining through her dining room window where Tom had claimed a spot in a convenient sunbeam. She set some paper on the table and went back to the kitchen, sawed off two thick slices of bread, buttered them with soft margarine, and poured herself another coffee with the water that had taken a dog's age to boil on the stove. Topping it up with a drop of Carnation Milk, she stared out the window at the bizarre sky.

She didn't know how long this emergency was going to last, but as mayor she was in charge. She flipped to the first page of the plan and began to read.

"Jesus, Tom," she glanced over at the lazy cat. "This is over the top. I have to secure the infrastructure, take inventory of all the food available in the houses and shops, and plan for planting. Surely this will be over before spring?"

The cat stared at her a second, decided her words weren't a signal that more food was forthcoming, and settled back into his sunbeam to give himself a good bath.

Resentment gnawed at Jean. The storm over, she had looked forward to just another ordinary day, puttering around. It was said the first casualty of war was truth, but Jean was beginning to think "ordinary" was the first to go. it had been damaged in recent years as the devastation from climate change tore nations apart and destroyed people's lives on every continent. Even here, where houses had been relocated to allow for the ever-rising ocean infringing on coastal properties, things had changed. The extreme weather had average summer temperatures at tropical levels, and a shark infestation that had wreaked havoc on fish stocks of all kinds. Yet they had adjusted. Markets for shark had opened and fishers had pivoted. The longer growing season saw agricultural benefits. The people who lived in Desolate were attached to the place and worked hard to see it survive when many rural communities were now rotted remnants of the old time of cold, dusty ghost towns that had succumbed to the ravages of the heated earth.

Jean read the entire booklet from start to finish before the council members arrived.

"Okay, Madame Mayor, let's call this meeting to order," Max said when all were assembled. "We got two away. Sam Jesso is gone to Gander to visit his father in the home and Mildred Marche is out with the flu. Sarah, are you ready for the minutes?"

At an affirmative from the town clerk, Jean cleared her throat. "I call this emergency meeting of the town council of Desolate Island to order."

Sarah noted the attendance, regrets, and the time. It was Ten am, March 12, 2047.

"We are in an emergency situation, " Joan began.

CHAPTER TWO

"What is happening? Does anybody have any idea? I heard that there was a big attack, and all the satellites are gone, that the US was attacked and that Russian submarines are in Canadian waters, even offshore Newfoundland." Maggie Rogers' voice shook, her expression somewhere between terror and delight. The first because she was a naturally fearful woman, the latter because this was the ultimate drama, something she thoroughly thrived on.

Max Dawe described her as "an infinitely stupid woman" to Jean when she first arrived in town, and she learned soon enough that it was more fact than opinion. Also, Max was known to be a highly intuitive, seventh son of a seventh son. He scoffed it off a lot after spending a lifetime being taunted for his 'magic', but if Max said something people listened. Plus, there was demonstrable proof of his assessment.

In Maggie's daily life, which contained no real employment, she busied herself with chickens. Her collection included an assortment of breeds, some nearly extinct, that were kept in what she called her sanctuary. She was particularly proud of her spitzhauben hens, the speckled, scrawny little creatures with tufts of feathers on their heads like pointy dunce hats. It was little more than a glorified hobby farm, but she busied herself selling eggs to locals and offering introductions of the chickens to the tourists that arrived every summer just to see rare birds. Inexplicably, the tourists loved it.

Maggie wouldn't have been on council if there had been an election. Her rare chickens were great for tourism, but her stupidity and negativity left her unpopular in the community. The gift of acclamation had made counselors out of many unpopular and incapable people in small places and Desolate Island was no different.

Her panic today was a bit more justified than the usual mink-in-the-henhouse drama and Jean felt less inclined to be annoyed at her.

"We can't panic," Jean said, a forced calm in her voice. "I've created an agenda for this meeting, but we have to maintain control of this situation, act with care and logic so we don't scare the town. We're out here all alone, in March. We have to take things easy. Figure out what we're dealing with."

"Mallory and Francis won't be happy," Max said.

"This will *distract from business*," Sarah Pomeroy grinned.

Everybody laughed, a welcome sound in the somber room. Jean, like the others, hated Mallory and Francis Richmond, owners of a small, local B&B they preferred to call an Inn. They had refurbished the rooms and fancied themselves town leaders, but Francis was an unmitigated asshole and Mallory was terrified of him. They had alienated nearly every member of the community with their airs about 'culinary' and 'haute cuisine'.

Once in a public meeting on the fishery, which had begun collapsing when numerous species began to die from the warming seas — salmon fishing was still outlawed despite record numbers, cod stocks were at record lows and sharks roamed the waters in large numbers — Frances had said that the time spent discussing developing markets for new fish species would *distract from business*. The statement had gotten him loud public jeers and he had grown red with anger at the reaction.

The fishery still accounted for thirty-five percent of the revenue that came to the small island community, with another fifty-eight percent coming from online work with A-Zon, the international conglomerate that employed people all over the world. People in places like Desolate could live modestly well off the eighteen dollar an hour minimum wage while in other areas it was nearly impossible.

But to Francis Richmond, the only business that mattered was tourism which, to be fair, had increased with his dogged determination to fill his *Posada Inn* with visitors. While it did add to the economy, bolstering the fishery did not in any way *distract from business*.

"You're being awful, but I'm curious how they'll take this distraction," Jean teased Sarah, and the mood lightened a bit.

"Let's get back to the agenda," Max encouraged, wanting to get out and do something as soon as he could.

They put their heads down and started assigning tasks according to the emergency plan and the agenda.

A while later, Jean looked around the room. "Okay, we've voted on the State of Emergency. We assume the province will call one too if this is that big, so we can get help from them if it's required. We'll call a public meeting later. But with this cold, and no electric heat, I think the priority is to turn off all the water in the public buildings including the town hall, the community center, school, and so on. It'll be a true disaster if the pipes freeze."

"Good idea. What about food spoilage?" Sarah stopped

typing on her A-Tab to ask.

"The shops have generators for their freezers, I figure. I'm going to leave my stuff in the freezer now so tell folks to do that. If the door stays closed, it should stay frozen for some while. If they think it's getting soft, put it outside, in their sheds. It's below the freezing point so it'll stay frozen out there."

"I heard on the news last week this cold spurt is supposed to last until next Tuesday," Maggie said.

"That's good then," Jean replied.

"May I say something?" Sarah Pomeroy asked. The town clerk didn't usually add much to the meeting.

"Go ahead, m'love." Jean smiled. Sarah was a sweet girl, smart as a whip and pretty like a daisy.

"What if we make a list of suggestions for everybody, then go door to door with them? If we could get the firemen and the council together, split up the town into sections, make everybody a copy of it, they could take it around along with a statement from the mayor about what is happening to get things going. The note from the mayor will reassure everybody."

"Good idea! What a pain not to be able to A-talk everybody," Jean said. "Glad I stocked up on paper. On the same list put an invite to the public meeting with the location and that way we'll get it all done in one go without having to retrace our steps."

"That's exactly what we need to do, good idea," Maggie agreed.

"Max, can you go get Reg to talk to the firefighters to turn off the water in the public buildings and if you think of any other measures to prevent damage, do that. Then bring them back here with you. Meanwhile, we'll work on a letter from me to send out. I'm going to bring in my generator and run the printer, so we can make a few copies. I know I should conserve fuel, but I think getting everybody together, keeping everybody calm, and making a plan is the priority right now. What say you all?"

The council members looked at each other and all nodded, their faces grave.

Jean smiled. "Now, 'tis not the end of the world. We'll get the Wi-Fi back," she joked.

"Will be the end of the world if me chickens freezes," Maggie said. Her eyes filled and she brushed at them with the back of her hand.

"Oh Maggie, I never thought about that. You have their coops heated normally, don't you?"

"Yeah, we have light bulbs in da coops to keep 'em warm."

Keeping those chickens alive was very important, Jean thought. If they were isolated for a very long time, the chickens and their eggs would be an important food source.

"Once the printing is done, you can have my generator to light those lights, Maggie."

Maggie's eyes brightened. "Really? That's wunnifow!" The old dialect was charming, a sign that the past thrived in this quaint place.

Jean's lips formed a tight smile. She wasn't being *wonderful*, though. She was being practical. One chop of a sharp axe and chickens were dinner.

The crowd left, and Jean took a moment to look out her window into the bright cold day. The peculiar hue of the easterly sky still bothered her. She suspected this wasn't a normal outage. She deduced that the war, long fought in foreign lands, had come to rest now upon their isolated, and highly vulnerable, shores. The only questions were, how bad was it and how long before it got to Desolate Island?

CHAPTER THREE

Jean made her way down the trail to the root cellar. The snow blower had made a nice pile on either side of the pathway, so it just needed a bit of shoveling to get it cleared this morning. She exhaled as she pulled the cellar door's handle, her breath a cloud of frigid mist rising from her lips and nose, dampening her warmed face as it stroked her skin.

The outer door gave after a good, two-handed tug, scraping snow along with its snug bottom. The interior latch opened without trouble. She shone the light from her otherwise useless phone into the cavernous vault.

The pungent odour of root vegetables and dirt drifted into the cold winter air and Jean wrinkled her nose while shining the light around, looking for spiders. Coast clear, she approached the potato bin first. There was a good supply if she were careful. She had plenty of turnips, and still a couple of five-gallon buckets of carrots in sawdust. Preservatives lined the shelves along the walls including beets, relish, pickles, carrots, mussels, and crab. She had been living nearly entirely off the bounty of the island for years.

"They won't be laughing at me now, if this trouble lasts a long time," Jean said to Tom, the cat, who followed her everywhere, guaranteeing a mouse-free cellar.

The locals had teased her often a decade earlier for moving from Toronto to their tiny island, living a hand to mouth existence while they traipsed off the ferry for nearly all their groceries. Most had freezers full of fresh fish and moose, but unlike her they didn't have a stock of the coveted dried, salted cod, racks of smoked salmon, a cellar of root vegetables and preserves of all kinds and enough toilet paper to last her for five years. She had a house pantry too, a converted spare bedroom, and in it she kept bags of flour, salt, sugar, baking ingredients, dried fruit, raisins, beans, lentils, rice, tea, coffee, and so on. She could survive for a long time on her stores. She grew greens and herbs in hydroponic beds inside and had even managed to raise two fruit-producing avocado trees in her living room. Her freezer held fresh cod and a supply of moose, shot and butchered by Max. She made jerky out of much of the meat and pickled another batch like salt beef, something Max considered a waste, preferring his moose in slivers with onions in a pan on the stove. She had a license and went along for the hunt as his partner, but he was the experienced shooter who did the killing.

She kept stores like this because she just didn't like leaving the island. She chose to, every few months for a trip, but her way of life was more like the traditional ways of the past than those whose family had occupied Desolate Island for generations.

"Why'd you come here anyway?" Reg, the town's fire chief had asked her about a year after she'd moved, a dangling cigarette stuck to his bottom lip like a tubular mole. It threatened to ignite the beard that didn't seem to ever grow any longer but never appeared to get trimmed either.

"Because it was cheap, and I was tired of the city," she'd answered. Jean had picked up the old salt box house for fifteen thousand dollars and spent another fifteen on ten acres of land in various locales throughout the town after just one visit.

People were anxious to sell but money was hard to come by and they had no further use for the abandoned fields with their long grasses dried and rotted in tangled bunches, vole-ridden and forgotten like their ancestors who had tilled it in years gone by.

"I grows enough for the winter but yoom gone crazy." He'd drawn on the smoke, handsfree, because it never left the corner of his mouth.

"I wanted an organic farm. This is perfect," she had added.

"Hard growin'."

"Not so hard anymore and it is good growing."

"You needs to flip these over tomorrow and let them dry. We got a spurt of good weather now, so you should be alright with 'em," he'd advised, referring to the flakes of fish she had 'made' under his guidance. She had cured the illegally caught cod in the sun every fall since after that first lesson, catching them herself by following the marks he'd shown her along with the method to catch them. He was one of only a handful who didn't use sonar and she'd loved learning from him as much as he loved sharing the nearly extinct knowledge. She risked massive fines, but the Feds barely bothered to come their way anymore, they were so busy monitoring coastal erosion and deadly sea surges that battered their shores with record intensity every year.

Sometimes she thought the town admired her for utilizing so many of their old ways. Most times she knew they considered her an interloper. But they still wanted her to be mayor because she was a good speaker and had brought some government projects and infrastructure to the town when things looked hopeless after the provincial government collapsed back in thirty-eight.

She wasn't the only one who farmed. A few others grew a bit too, and then there was Maggie and her chickens that brought the tourists in. That was a hobby, though, and Maggie only sold the eggs, the colourful birds kept as pets. The woman cried to break her heart when the delicate creatures keeled over dead. Sometimes she even took a hen-pecked straggler into her house if the others plucked too many feathers off it.

Jean backed out of the cellar, gallon bucket in hand filled over the top with pradies, as Rex called them, and a turnip.

Food wasn't an issue for her, not yet, but it might become one for many.

The red glow on the horizon to the east caught her attention again. She sniffed. A harsh, smoky odour floated in the air, somewhat like that of a struck match. Something was burning somewhere, and a veer in the wind would send more smoke their way although the ocean was the best firebreak any town could wish for.

How she loved it here. Sometimes when the last ferry left at night, Jean sat in her house enveloped in a monumental peace. She'd knit, or work on a quilt, alone in the quiet, lights out except for the one that shone on her handiwork, grateful for fate landing her in this safest of all places.

Now though, for the first time since moving to Desolate Island, the isolation felt like entrapment and her sense of peace deserted her. She walked up to her bridge, stomping her feet to shake off both the snow and a strange sense of loss. She yanked on the door that always stuck when it was cold and stepped inside, setting the bucket of vegetables on a bench. The heat from the kitchen stove welcomed her. She stripped off her coat and mittens, hung them on the rack then kicked off her boots.

Hands extended, she moved towards the stove, hovering them over its antique surface. She felt a bit smug about this appliance, had searched for it for ages, paid a fortune for it and to have it shipped, then set up in the kitchen by Reg, the fire chief who shook his head the whole time he worked. He admired its beauty but scoffed that she hadn't bought a modern pellet stove for heat or at least a normal wood stove, since these old things were inefficient and a waste of time.

But unlike other woodstoves, she could cook on this, and the heat, while not as even as electric, still worked in a pinch. The oven required some experimentation, but it too, functioned for cooking and baking. Plus, it warmed the kitchen, bathroom, and bedroom provided she left the oven, and all other doors open and closed off the living room. Wood was pricey, the tree protection act of 2025 forcing every tree cut to be replaced and exorbitant fines for offenders meant wood was pricey — unless you know the right people. Again, in this isolated place, nobody bothered the tree poachers any more than they did the cod poachers. Surely the few trees lopped down on Desolate Island weren't all that important in the carbon reduction plan, Jean told herself whenever a twinge of guilt made its way into her consciousness.

She pulled a junk of birch out from the tray, opened the round lid, and stuffed it in, enjoying the crackle of the flaming rind before she closed it up.

Tom leapt up and flopped down on the futon, cocked one leg in the air, and started licking himself, twisting his head as his rough tongue pulled through fur that had been cleaned just as thoroughly an hour before.

He paused when the knock came, as did Jean. Not that she needed to move. Max opened the door and stepped inside without even his courtesy knock.

"Jean, I got news. Did you have the radio on?"

"No, I was out in the cellar and I'm trying to save batteries anyway. What is it?"

He shook his head, as though to clear some thoughts, to make room for hard words. His red-rimmed eyes squared off with hers and he slipped off his hat, holding it in front of his chest like a shield. Then, he spoke with a voice low and cracked, drenched in the dialect of the people who had settled this island two hundred years before. "Oh, dear Jesus, she's Goddamned gone, b'y, she's all Goddamned gone. She's all gone—"

Then, unable to speak further, the eighty-odd year-old man hung his head down and wept.

CHAPTER FOUR

"What's all gone?" Jean pulled the distraught man forward. Max was as spry as she was and tough as boot leather. Now, though, he was ashen, his face grey and drawn and his eyes red.

"She's all gone, Jean. They blew up the Avalon."

"What?" She sat. Then stood. She moved to the stove, lifted the lid, and put the stove-top kettle over the open flame shooting out the top. It didn't dawn on her to doubt him as unbelievable as his words were.

"Was it a nuclear bomb? Bombs?"

"Might be nuclear, I think 'tis, but I don't know, but they was hit by something. And Gander too. Everything on the east coast. They razed it all."

"Oh fuck." Jean sat, almost flattening Tom who shifted over a bit.

"The rest of the country is fine. For now, but we're on fire. Fires would be worse if there wasn't snow, but you know they don't have any snow on the Avalon anymore. They says a bunch of people from the Gander area is gone towards Lewisporte, because though it's close, it wasn't blown up."

"Who did it?"

"Nobody knows, but they figure the target was the

Americans."

"I knew we shouldn't have let them in."

"We couldn't stop them. They're allies."

"They're a target and by being in this province they made us one." American warships were everywhere in Newfoundland waters. It was a strategically sensible location for them since the war started. There were troops in massive new bases set up in both Gander and St. John's. Well, there had been. Christ.

"That red glow, that's Gander?" Jean walked to the kitchen window. The eerie orange light was not as bright but still burned.

"I think it must be." Max followed her, looking out.

Desolate was several hours drive from Gander. Then there was a half hour ferry ride.

"If it's the atomic bomb, we'll probably get some radiation." Jean's voice trembled.

"You think?" His somber voice shook as well.

"They're all gone. Everybody in Gander? If that was nuclear... Sam Jesso—does Daphne know?" The town councillor had gone to Gander.

"She does, refuses to believe it. And everybody in St. John's, for sure," Max repeated.

Jean remembered then. "Your family, Max?" He had sons, one in St. John's, the other in Toronto.

"If it's gone, he's gone." His bottom lip quivered, and his red-rimmed eyes filled. Turned out crying wasn't a skill that required practice, Max thought. He had not cried since he was a boy, but they flowed with ease, washing down his crinkled cheeks. He didn't bother wiping them away.

"They're all gone. All those people." Jean's stomach clenched. She sat, then stood, then sat again. Then finally she went to put the kettle on the stove only to find she'd already done it.

"Or injured, burned. I remember the pictures of the people burned in Vietnam. And where will the injured go? The doctors would be gone too, the hospital. I can't even think about it. Better to be gone straight away."

Jean's mind darted to a memory of a friend, Mary Bursey. She was shopping at Walmart, Jean's cart loaded up with enough cat food to last for a year because it was on sale. Mary had been shopping with her little boy when they'd met in the aisle. They'd elbow thumped, a greeting leftover from the twenties pandemic era, and Jean asked how she was making out this winter. The child, Luke, sat in the basket of the cart, a tad overweight, cheeks red, nose dripping with the cold that his mother said he'd had for months. His dye-stained lips from a green ring lollipop on his middle finger had formed into a sticky smile as he offered her a taste.

"I'll pass," Jean had said that day, his sticky face crestfallen for a second before he nodded his head and went back to work on it, the green spit dripping down his chin, rivulets of sugary innocence. Good Lord, she should have at least pretended to taste it. That poor family. Gone.

Had the bomb hit at night? When everyone slept so that they were sent to cinder in their slumber? Unaware. And what of the injured? They would be burned. They would be sick. Radiation poisoning. And what were they facing on Desolate Island? She never wanted Google so badly.

"Wait? Maybe it isn't true! Why didn't we hear it?" Jean asked. "Those things are loud. I know we're clear across the province, but don't you think we would have heard it?"

"The storm. We had the storm. It was raging out here, so loud we didn't hear anything, and the wind was in their direction."

"Damn. That's right. But on the east coast, they didn't get the storm." Jean looked down at the kettle, watching the steam rise from its spout.

"It's all over. The world is ending, Jean. I suppose I thought I'd die before I seen the end of the world."

"It hasn't ended yet. We're still here. Glad you have your sense of humour about you though. Gives me hope."

"What kind of hope though? We've got Armageddon. I knew when America fell. When they were took over by— "

"The kettle is boiled. Let's stay calm. Have a cup of tea. What else do you know? Is that it?" God knows that was enough.

"What they're saying is that it's all out nuclear war. I don't know who is fighting who, or who even started it. The radio station is not even official, just some journalists who have it set up. They said nuclear bombs are going off everywhere."

"Christ almighty. What are we supposed to do?" Jean poured boiling water into a teapot and threw in a tea bag.

"We're doomed. Perhaps 'tis better to have the bomb dropped on our heads right off than to starve to death out here."

"Or perhaps we can survive out here."

"If they stop the bombing. We're already dead as far as I'm concerned, we just haven't had a chance to lay down yet." He took his tea, his wrinkled hand shaking.

"We have the generator running at the school so we

can have the public meeting there. We have to tell everybody what's going on." Jean pulled up a chair.

"Do you think they'll panic? I think they'll go nuts."

"I don't know but I have a feeling we'll be needing a guard on the cellar," Jean said.

"I got a bolt action pump gun and a three aught three. Anybody comes 'longside 'er," Max threatened.

"Get Turrs, Max. Get some ducks. Seals. Shoot whatever you want. Got a feeling DFO isn't going to be monitoring the bag count anymore."

"No more DFO, uh? Well, that's one Goddamned silver lining." He blew across the steaming mug and sipped his tea, heart full of pain for a son likely gone and a province in ruins.

CHAPTER FIVE

"Max, one of the recommendations in the plan is that we should combine our households to save on heating requirements. I know this is weird, but I really feel you should come over with me. Shut your place up. I've a ton of space. Are you okay for medicine?"

Max lived hand to mouth, his pension barely covering his costs. Like many, he still used the costly Cleanfuel that most inhabitants in remote places used. It was heavily controlled and subsidised for Max, a low-income senior with no other heating option. Few people had stores. Plus, he was diabetic and took pills for that. She hoped he had enough. Who could guess how long it would be before a shipment of either could be brought into the island. She had plenty of wood and stores herself and only the two of them lived here on the point. He wouldn't get a pension if mail wasn't coming, or the computers couldn't deposit it to his bank.

"Too soon to make big decisions," Max said.

"Well, make a small one then. Come over at least until we get things figured out. I could use your help around here. Keeping the stove going for one thing. Everything is manual now." She knew that he'd help her in a second but wouldn't take charity in a lifetime.

"I just got groceries. I would have to bring stuff over, so it won't freeze."

"Much in the freezer?"

"No, not much."

"Do you have fuel?"

"Know what I 'as?" Max asked, eyes alight with an idea, the 'h' dropped of his 'has'. But she knew the quirks of the dialect now and understood.

"What?"

"I has five kerosene lamps and a five gallon bucket of kerosene," Max told her, the 'h' miraculously reappearing.

"Well, bring them over and we'll have light. Let's do all that after the meeting. Are you able to walk there? I can drive but I don't want to use the car unless I have to." She had plugged her phone into the car to charge it. The car battery was also fully charged but it wouldn't take long to use that up. She was ever hopeful there would be a return of mobile service or Wi-Fi and she wanted to be ready for it, if so.

Jean walked close to Max. He was sure on his feet but there was a weakness in him she'd not seen once in her decade of being his neighbour. He was aware that one son might be dead or injured and the grief of it aged him the way ten years hadn't.

***

They alighted the door of the packed gym. Every able adult in town was in the room, a few small babies as well but no children. They might talk of things too much for children to handle and it was best to leave them in the care of the older kids.

All eyes looked at her. She offered a brief smile. Nothing could prepare her for such a role. Leadership of a small community that needed a funding application for a water system or writing a letter of support for local business people for growth funds, that was her talent. She could bring money in. She wasn't sure she could bring in what they needed now, even if she could figure out what it was.

She'd certainly spent enough of her own money having employed many of the locals to work on her house, rebuild the root cellar, clear the land, and help harvest the vegetables in the fall. She breathed, looking deep inside herself for guidance. What did she know about them? What did they want from her? No, *need* from her.

God, these people were good. They were so very good.

Her mind drifted back to a time several years earlier when she'd traveled to a wedding in Hawaii. Midway through the reception a call came in from Reg, the fire chief, who had the spare key to her place.

"I put all your stuff in your living room. Then we got some ropes and tied it all to the land, so you should be good," he'd said without preamble.

"What do you mean, Reg?" Margarita in hand, she waited for his answer as she looked out over the bright blue Pacific.

"Well, a starm is ragin'. Surge is wicked. We lost the Blake's stage and a couple more looks ready to go, so me and a few of the fullers thought we'd latch yours on. But in case it doesn't work, we put all your stuff in the house."

"Thank you." Jean translated in her mind the words storm and fellows. Her disbelief had her unable to say more.

"I got to go, we got a few more to save. Didn't want

you to worry is all." He spoke as though it was nothing.

"It's still storming there?" Finally she'd found her voice.

"Oh yes, not fit. We tie ourselves on though so we won't blow into the cove."

"Be careful," Jean warned and had hung up with another thank you. She'd opened the weather network App and typed in her new hometown. The warning called for gusts of 130km/h winds. They really were tying themselves on and then tethering the buildings to the land. It had worked too. The ropes had held her stage when several shores and spanners were knocked out and that spring a group of them came and re-shored it with *sticks* that they sawed themselves. She tried to pay them for that work, but they scoffed at the idea.

Now they were looking to her to do some saving. Give them something to hang on to. Shore them up in some way. The most she could hope for was to alleviate their fears. How the hell could she do that if she was terrified as hell herself?

The council lined up chairs on stage. She climbed the steps on the right and they followed her, nervous. They sat while she walked to the podium. "Hello everybody." The folder in her hand shook.

The crowd mumbled a greeting and kept on talking. Reg, the fire chief, raised a hand, coming forward. His loud voice carried to the back of the hall and when he shouted, "Hey!" The room quietened. "We don't have the PA system, so we need it quiet. If everybody can take a seat. Mrs. Roberts needs a chair, somebody." He pointed to the elderly woman who was directed to a seat vacated by a younger woman who smiled and moved to lean against the wall.

"I'm going to tell you what I know. Like Reg said, we don't have a mic so I'm going to bawl at you all," Jean said, using their word for shout. There was a general laugh. She waited for the room to get quiet again. "Then I'm going to let you ask questions. If I can answer I will, but odds are I won't be able to. So here it is. The war has escalated. From what we can tell, the entire eastern US and Canada, Newfoundland precisely, has been hit. We know St. John's and Gander was. We don't know what they were hit with, but we suspect atomic bombs."

A woman's sob escaped somewhere around the third row, and some murmurs of consolation were whispered. Jean knew that nearly everybody in the room had friends or family in Gander or on the Avalon. She didn't see Daphne Jesso in the crowd. Shame coiled in her belly. She didn't think she could handle a heartbroken widow right now but that was nothing compared to a woman becoming one. She drew a deep breath and exhaled before speaking again.

"I'm not going to sugar coat this. I know some of you have lost people today or think you have. I am so sorry. I don't even quite know what to say. But my responsibility is to take care of you people. To advise you. For now, as horrible as this is, we're safe and alive. We must take steps to make sure we stay that way. At least until we get more information. Reg?"

He came forward. Jean stepped aside, while he read out the details of the plan as they had arranged.

"Double up wherever possible. If everybody shared homes and food, then that would cut down on the use of our limited fuel and wood until we can get more."

"I've got an extra room in my house," Jean offered. "Max is coming over with me. But I do have another if anybody is in need."

An arm went up from the third row. It was the woman who had cried.

"I want to come up with you if I can bring my cat and the baby. My load of wood didn't come and while I can stand the cold, my girl, I wouldn't want her cold. She might get sick."

"Yes, you can come to my place, Lydia. I'd love to have you." Lydia Woodruff was raising her grandchild. Her daughter, an addict, lived in St. John's. Several years back, the landlady called the police when she went by to collect rent and heard a wailing child. She'd used her master key and found the two-month-old, red-faced, in a pile of her own feces, screaming with hunger and from the pain of the sores that spotted her tiny bottom.

Children's aid brought the child to Lydia who did her best, but she had terrible rheumatoid arthritis that left her partially blind. Now her daughter was most likely dead. That must have been why she'd sobbed from the third row.

The room got loud again, people discussing what to do, disagreeing, and sometimes crying.

"Look, I knows you're the mayor, but I don't want to go in with nobody else and I don't want nobody in with me. I got wood enough to get me through and I got grub in 'til we get the pension and can get some more." Gus Rideout stood, the defiance in his thrust chin dared her to disagree.

"Gus, I'm not telling you what to do, I'm just making suggestions."

"Shut up, Gus, sit down," Lorraine Franklin snapped at him. "We know you won't help nobody and nobody wants you to anyway, let the mayor speak."

The crowd started to grumble, arguing back and forth. Most of them in defense of her. She called for order, but the chatter continued.

A loud whistle shot through the room from somewhere in the back. The crowd went quiet. RJ Drake gave her a thumbs-up, leaned back against the wall, and winked.

"Thanks, RJ. Never learned how do to that in my misspent youth." She looked back at the crowd. "Look everyone, I'm not going to tell you what to do. You get to decide, but I'm going to give you all a reality check. First, there will be no cheques. No Canadian Guaranteed Income Benefit, no Canada Pension, no deposits from A-Zon to access, no mail of any kind, no banking of any kind if the major centres of this province have been destroyed. Second, there is nowhere to get supplies. The ferry isn't running — can't run, at least for now. What we have currently is what we have. Figure out, on paper, how much Cleanfuel you have, how much food you have. The shopkeepers, you need to figure out what your stores are. We've several hundred people to feed here and we need to preserve what is here and figure out how to get enough for another year."

"Another year? You think this is going to last a year?" Garland Roberts put his hand on his mother's shoulder.

"What about tourists?" another voice added. It sounded like Francis Richmond.

"Tourists? Are you nuts? There's not going to be any tourists, the province is blown to bits. We'll probably all die from radiation. There won't be any tourists or A-Zon. This is Armageddon for God's sakes." RJ spoke up from the back of the room. Several men jumped up and made their way towards him. Lydia started to cry again, and the council stood, moving behind Jean.

Reg yelled, "Stop," but they kept on going. RJ put two fingers in his mouth and the sharp whistle silenced the room again. This time, however, he made his way forward, towards the stage. A hand reached out and grabbed him as he passed but he yanked away and took the steps in two strides to stand by Jean.

"I'll keep 'em quiet for you. But tell them the full truth. You kept the youngsters out for a reason, didn't you?"

Jean nodded. Then started to speak again, grateful for his support. He was right. There was some serious denial here. "Gar, I don't know anything for sure except we should plan for the worse and hope for the best. And RJ here is one hundred percent right. If what we're hearing on the news is accurate, we're on our own and what we have is what we have. We need to save it, spare it along. Reg wants to do an inventory of ammunition. There are seals around we can kill for food, for example."

"I won't be wasting a bullet on a seal. I'll kill 'em the old way, with a whack on the head," Reg said. The room laughed and agreed. Jean tried not to look too shocked.

"Anybody goes swilin' let me know. I'll come with you," RJ offered.

"We needs somebody to watch the wind if you goes off for swiles. I read they always rung the church bell to let the men know if it went off land so they could come in," Reg replied using the old word for seals that few did anymore.

"Looks like we're going to live like they did in the good old days," Jean said.

"The good old days were Goddamned awful," Max remarked. There were nods from several of the seniors.

"But better than this," a quiet voice spoke from the front." Can we pray?" old Mrs. Roberts asked.

"Would you lead us?" Jean asked. And the older woman nodded, the task one she'd done many times, having been the lay minister of the Anglican Church for many years. Roy Pearcey, the current lay reader, looked a bit put-out at her request, but he held back, said nothing. He'd have lots of time to preach. Disaster always filled pews in his experience.

"Dear Lord, we've come upon troubled times," she began, grey head bowed, eyes closed, withered hands clasped around a hand carved cane.

Understatement of the century, Jean thought, her head lowered, eyes closed too, an atheist with a 'just in case' mentality. We're probably all going to die, she thought.

In the next instant she felt death was upon her as a large bang reverberated throughout the crowded gymnasium.

CHAPTER SIX

"We got people coming on the ice," Jeremy Marche said, his twelve-year-old eyes as broad as dinner plates.

"Jeremy, what are you doing here? You were supposed to bide home." His mother, Delphine Marche jumped to go to him, embarrassed that he had frightened them all so much when the door slammed.

"Mom, Emily said I should come. We looked out and they're coming. A big, long string of people."

The crowd grew loud, questioning the boy, then looking back and forth at each other, asking, speculating.

"Come up, Jeremy," Jean invited. "Tell us what you saw." A few of the men left to see for themselves what the boy was talking about.

"Mrs. Adler, they are on the ice up a-ways yet but looks like they came across from the mainland." His young voice was still pre-adolescent and dialect aside, he spoke loud and clear and his voice carried to the back walls.

"They can't cross the run, it's broke open." She looked to Max to clarify.

"Well, the ferry hasn't run now for, what, three days? And it was vicious cold, so perhaps the ice is jammed together, froze solid enough," RJ said, pushing his long hair back and replacing his hat.

"How many, Jeremy?" Jean asked.

"Emily counted forty through the spyglasses," he answered.

"We can't add that many people to the town, we can't feed more people," Gus said.

"We'll do what we can for them, but let's see what we're dealing with first," Jean replied.

"Maybe we should go out on the ice to meet them," RJ suggested.

"I think you're right. It's what? At least ten kilometers from the mainland? They would have walked a long time in the cold." Jean also wondered what had driven them to do such a dangerous thing.

"Jeremy, you go on home," Delphine admonished, but Jean smiled at him. "Thanks for coming to tell us. You did well."

He beamed, and then: "Is we at war Mrs. Adler?"

"I think we must be. But we don't know for sure."

"Okay, we gonna help those people now?" He nodded as though his affirmative gesture could create her yes. Boy would be a great salesman when he grew up. *If* he grew up.

Oh, God. Stop that, Jean, she told herself. "Yes of course, we'll do our best," she said.

"I hope you don't think we're going to put up those people?" Francis Richmond yelled.

The thought had crossed her mind. There were empty rooms at the inn.

"Francis. That is up to you. We'll bring them to the gym first, see what we decide. We need to work as a team. Help where we can, but everybody has the right to do what they want."

"We are not taking them. I don't believe this anyway.

We don't have any kind of proof that things won't get back to normal. People have been afraid of this war for a long time, but the south China Sea and Europe are a long way from this place."

"You're a selfish old bugger, Francis," RJ said.

"Shut up!" Francis moved forward, and RJ jumped off the stage and headed down the centre aisle in his direction.

Jean watched, appalled, but mesmerized. All eyes followed as he approached Francis, eager for a racket, hoping to see Francis flattened by the younger, fitter man. RJ slowed down as he passed but didn't stop.

"You're an arsehole, Francis. I'm going to go get rigged out to go meet those people. I think we can bring them up on the point by the mayor's house. You go home, I wouldn't put a dog I didn't like in your fancy B and fuckin' B."

It was a deliberate jab. Francis always emphasized they were an Inn, not a B&B as though the latter was far beneath him.

The crowd folded in behind RJ, inspired to follow. Jean stood on the stage, buttoned her sealskin coat, perplexed but pleased somehow, before she followed her people.

"We best get over to the point, see what's coming," RJ said when she caught up to him.

"Okay. Thanks for that back there. It helped."

"Yeah, no problem. Here comes Max now."

"Here, let me help you with that." She grabbed the scarf from Max as she struggled to wind it around his neck.

The wind blustered against their faces as they walked. RJ launched ahead of them, hopped on his snowmobile and was off. He was at her house when she got there, skidoo running as they approached.

"Go on in, b'y," she encouraged as Max split off from her, going to his place to start bringing stuff over.

"Shut it off, can't waste fuel. Come on." She indicated the snowmobile, then the house.

He did as he was told.

"Miss Adler, I didn't mean to interrupt your meeting—," RJ looked around at her kitchen, his intense eyes taking in everything.

"You helped. And it's Jean. Tell me, what are you thinking about this?"

"Look, I know everybody thinks I'm pretty useless around town." He pulled off his cap, long blond hair falling around his face.

"Yes, you have a certain, um, reputation." Jean grinned.

"I know. My own fault, but anyway. Where are your binoculars?"

Jean went to get them and pondered what she'd heard about her guest. RJ held several degrees, had hooked up with a good paying job, quit after just a short while working, returned, and remained. He fished and poached wood with his father but mostly he drank beer and hung out playing darts and pool all winter. He had no ambition and no drive which was strange, considering he'd escaped. He could have been working in St. John's teaching or whatever he'd trained for.

When there was a St. John's.

The cold air in the living room when she opened the door caught Jean off guard. A shiver ran through her. The Bishnell binoculars were located and brought to RJ who adjusted them. He looked through them out her window. After a few moments, he nodded and handed them back.

"Over towards Ragged Island." He pointed to guide her.

She peered through, moved left to right, then back. Only white filled her view and she adjusted and searched for a contrast. Nothing. Then she focused closer, looking slightly downward on the black streak through the middle that looked like clear water by comparison but was in fact, a grey shade of the blanched expanse. There they were, antlike, trudging across the ice field. She could make out children huddled with parents, couples holding hands, babies hauled on sleighs. They dragged loaded toboggans. There were no skidoos which was odd. Some had guns slung over their shoulders. Her heart jumped at that. For hunting, nothing more... she hoped.

"They're close to the rent now," she whispered, referring to the gap of ice in the trail broken by the ferry.

"I think it's solid enough, but we can't be sure." RJ's voice was deep near her ear.

"I don't think I can watch. Jeez, RJ, kids. What if they fall through? We can't lose them."

"We gotta get out there. You want to come on skidoo with me? I'll hook up the cart, we can take some blankets out. It's still minus twelve and with the wind—"

"Yeah, do that."

"Dress as warm as you can."

"Grab this." She pulled a black, plastic garbage bag out, opening it up, inviting him to hold it abroad. When he did, she grabbed several quilts, some extra hats and mitts, tossing it all in until the bag was full.

"I'll take the car to the end of the point. Meet me there when you get the sled hooked on."

RJ agreed and fifteen minutes later a trail of ski-doos met them.

"They're going to try to cross. If they lay on their bellies, disperse their weight, they might make it. We need to get out there, help them," Reg said. The heaving of the sea under the floes made the entire situation tenuous. A lift of tide could crack the entire area wide open in any moment.

"We'll do what we can, and we'll take care of them, if they make it across," Jean replied.

"We'll all have one rider on our skidoos except RJ if he takes the mayor here," Reg said to the gathered team. "We're only going to the edge of the rent, but we got some rails on the sleds, so we can reach out if somebody does fall through. We got ropes too, just in case." Reg hauled a black balaclava down over his face. Jean pulled hers down too. Face and eyes caps, they called them here. They protected your face while letting your eyes see, so she supposed it made some sense. Nobody wore helmets. Nobody noticed.

"Get on, misses," RJ invited, patting the seat of his snowmobile.

Jean hung on to the sides as he eased the machine down over the bank onto the ice, sleds rattling behind them. They were the old-fashioned type built in two parts, joined by chains and used to haul out wood. RJ's snowmobile was a heavy-duty machine, great for sport and even better for hard work. It lifted and fell over the bumps made by the craggy edges of the Labrador ice-pans, welded together with water, frost, and snow.

They picked up speed as they came close to the rest of the team, coming to a stop a short distance from the shiny ice frozen between the chalky white floes. Jean stepped off the snowmobile and walked near the edge to stand next to Reg. The walkers faced them and waved from the other side. They waved back.

"Get on your bellies," Reg shouted. They couldn't tell for sure if those on the other side heard, so he grabbed a rail, tossed it across the ice in front of himself and lowered to his belly and made his way partly across the surface to demonstrate.

They waved again, shouting okay and yes across the broad expanse.

Soon the walkers became crawlers, inching forward, using their arms, like soldiers between trenches, men first to make sure it was safe, but the little kids moved faster than the adults so that the first across was a young girl, face covered in scarves. There was a loud cheer as she grabbed the long pole and Reg pulled her to safety.

Jean helped her stand, and she was taken away by another person. RJ and Jean flattened onto their bellies then and reached with the rails towards the next to make it across.

A sound travelled across the ice floes to Jean, a hissing noise that was difficult to hear amidst the shouts as people ice-swam forward at the encouragement of the others. Soon it morphed into something identifiable, no longer hiss but a cracking of the ice. The sound was of air being released as it was freed from beneath the surface by the pressure of the people on the thin sheets that traversed the gap. Jean looked around. Nobody seemed to be noticing it, so she carried on, determined to get the people across fast. Just in case.

A man's face was soon pulled close to hers. He grinned as he rolled and sat up.

"Thank you," he said, then turned around immediately to take over for her, to help his people get across quickly.

One by one, hands grasped the poles, allowing themselves to be pulled to the safety of the solid floes, the strange hiss-crack like a demon warning them their fate was not yet sealed.

After what seemed like hours, the last person was pulled to safety and Jean's breath left her body in a whoosh.

RJ chuckled. "That was stressful, eh?"

"All too stressful. It was cracking. I thought, oh God." Tears filled her eyes, she dashed them away. "Could you hear it?"

"Yeah. But it didn't break. Guess a few cracks mean nothing much now." He lodged an arm around her shoulder for a moment. "Let's finish up and get these people to warmth."

The ice-walkers chatted together with their rescuers. The surface beneath them heaved and the rent behind them cracked under the strain of the water beneath and the melded ice floes on either side. They all turned as one just in time to see the trail cave in and a gaping hole form in the very centre of the icey run.

"Oh, God, let's get out of here!" someone shouted.

Jean stood upright, her forearms tired from hauling the rails forward with a weary human hanging on. A woman hugged her briefly and Jean let her. The pandemics were long over and what did they matter now anyway?

One by one they were given rides back, a couple of the children sitting at the front of snowmobiles, tucked in behind the visor and out of the wind. Others hugged each other or sat, legs over the sides, on the poles across the sleds. And the rest walked fast away from the sinkhole behind them that had nearly swallowed them all whole.

"We're from Green Harbour, I'm Colin," a man with

ice frozen into his beard, said, getting close to Jean. "We made for here when the soldiers came."

"I'm the mayor, Jean Adler. What soldiers?" Jean's sealskin covered elbow met his in greeting.

"Oh, you call into On Air sometimes, don't you?" He said, referring to a local call-in radio show.

"Yes. On occasion. There are soldiers?" she repeated her question.

"Yes, they took our snowmobiles and cars. They moved into our houses, took right over. Lots of people stayed, said they're Americans so they're on our side but we didn't trust them, so we packed up what we could and left."

"They didn't try to stop you?"

"No, they said we'd freeze on the ice. They would have stopped us p'raps if they knew we took food, but we hid that away first. We don't have a lot, but we got some. And medicine. I took everything from the pharmacy. Can we get the people into the warm? The youngsters been walking for a long time. We can help cut some wood to help out. We have a cutting permit. You know you have lots of wood out here with the no cutting regulations you guys always had."

He had no way of knowing about the wood poachers and she wasn't about to tell him. The shame of cutting a tree without permission was massive, though she doubted anybody would care as much as they would have a day ago.

Jean started directing people as soon as they were all back on shore. "Get folks to bring blankets and warm clothes. We'll billet them off to different houses from the school."

An older woman shivered. A quilt was wrapped over

her.

"Do we have anybody hurt?" she asked Colin.

"Might have frostbite but nothing more. Lucky the ice froze over." He glanced in the direction of the shattered surface.

"I say, lucky the storm stopped the ferry and it had a few days to freeze. Otherwise, you'd be stuck over there. Come on, let's go."

"Lucky you came to help us across. We never would have made it on our own." Colin followed her. He was the leader of his group, she the leader of hers. He needed her allyship, and he hoped she needed his.

The crowd in the school was animated when they arrived. Jean tried not to trouble herself about the amount of Cleanfuel being used to warm the old gym.

"Thirty-seven," RJ approached them.

Reg shook his head. "What will we do with all of them? Set up beds here?"

"Let's see what the mayor says," RJ replied.

Jean was on the stage. "We're going to accommodate all of you," she said. "But we need to figure it all out. One of our visitors is a registered nurse. That's good since our nurse was caught off the island when this started. Visitors, you're in the hands of the experts now. These are the Anglican women's group. They'll figure out places for you all to stay, get you fed, and sorted out."

"We'll take care of everything, Mrs. Adler," an elderly lady who ran the local church said with a nod of her determined head.

"I know you will, Claire. Now this is important. Remember we are in a state of emergency. So, we're going to have to ration the use of all Cleanfuel, wood, and well, any kind of fuel. If you don't have enough wood to heat your house for a few months, get together with your neighbours. Share. Cut what you need, forget the old cutting laws, but keep in mind, chainsaws burn Cleanfuel too. One more thing, because we have no phones, we're going back to some old-fashioned communication. So, if you hear the Anglican church bells ring and a pause, then three times and a pause, all adults come to the gym right away. If you hear it ring straight through, with no pauses, everybody come. That means the elderly, children, everybody. Understand?"

Solemn faces nodded.

Jean turned around and noticed most of the men who helped in the rescue were gone. "Where did everyone go?" Jean asked.

"They saw some seals on the way back, so they're gone to pick off a few," Claire said.

Jean hoped they'd been joking about the knocks on the head. She was relieved when she heard the first gunshot. "Make sure I get some flippers, Claire," she said to the chair of the church women group as she left the school in her capable hands.

CHAPTER SEVEN

The sky darkened and a strange orange glow simmered in the distance. The large window at the west side of the kitchen afforded a view of the sunset that brightened with an ominous light. Fires still burned, but less so. Either that or the smoky odour in the air had decreased as the wind blew it in the opposite direction.

An obnoxious pale-yellow clock tick-tocked on the counter. Jean had pulled the old thing from a drawer in the spare bedroom, setting it with an anxious twist of the winding key. She let out a breath when it began to mark the minutes, as though she feared that without doing so, time would somehow cease.

Time was a nebulous concept at best. Slippery like an eel. A lifetime was nothing but a few heartbeats in the ages, but everything to the heart's owner. Each tick reminded Jean that her heart still pumped blood in her veins even if she could no longer identify a purpose for her life beyond surviving each percussion. Normal no longer existed, dissipated like the atoms of ten-thousand people, ashes to ashes, dust to dust. One day there, the next day not even a memory, all who knew them blown into oblivion at their sides.

All the great innovations and technology that had diminished the isolation of this lonely place had been annihilated. Not even television remained although it had gone the way of the dinosaur years before anyway, replaced by streaming. No N-Stream or AI assistance from the A-Zon. No A-Zon devices at all. In fact, there was barely radio. The outside world had as good as vanished.

They were alone. Desperate souls huddled on a rock, in a darkness that was worse than the absence of light. It was the dark of unknowing. Jean shook her head as though to free it of maudlin thoughts.

RJ was a comfortable stranger. She turned to him, away from the clock.

"I can't uninvite Lydia after promising to take her and Ashlyn, but Max has agreed to stay here and let a family stay at his place. So, he's coming here, and they're staying there, which is odd but that's the plan. I think Max needs company and not that of strangers, though he'd never admit that. I have the futon and I can set up a bedroom in the living room if I have to. I've been keeping the door closed but if I open it up, it'll warm enough, I think. I can light the old parlour stove at night as well. Reg said he'll check the chimney, make sure it's sound. I've not used it in years. I can accommodate one person or a couple perhaps. I'll do my best."

She looked to him for answers because there was nowhere else to look.

"The crowd staying at Max's brought food, not sure how much but they just needed a house. He has nothing there but half a week's worth," RJ said. Then he added, "What if I come here? I've set up a family in our house with Dad. Now there's not much room for me."

"Your dad going to go for that?" RJ's father, Ralph Drake Sr., never left his house except to fish or go in the woods. Painfully shy, it was the late June Drake who RJ had inherited his personality from. His looks too. His dark hair and intense blue eyes all came from her.

"He did. Well, he agreed to the family. They can do more for him than me. Dad needs medicine. Once he runs out, I don't know what we'll do, but Colin, the father, is a registered nurse. I gave him and his wife my room, the kids the spare and I was to take the couch." Staying here, on Jean's futon was a good plan. Aside from it being more comfortable, of all the people on the island, other than Francis at the B&B and the shop, Jean had the most supplies. That was an advantage too.

"Okay, so you and Max come here. Max will stay in the back room. I'll organize that for him. Lydia and the little girl in the bigger room, you in the parlour on the futon. Francis won't take even one family?"

"He never even came back to the school." RJ's eyes flashed with anger.

"Arse, eh?" Jean drained her cup of tea. "Help me get this place set up then. God, Lydia and Ashlyn's place isn't fit for either of the families. I didn't even offer it up. The wind blows the snow right into the bedroom. I didn't know it was so bad as it is until today. I hope it's warm enough for you in there. This house is well insulated, had it gutted and restored when I bought it so it's sound but still, two wood stoves aren't much heat."

"I visited Lydia's a while back. It was stark, like living in a fishing stage. This will be fine. Between us we'll drive up the heat." RJ winked at her. "Come on, let's get the room ready."

Twenty minutes later, it was cleared out. "Good Lord, this is heavy." Jean hauled the mattress over on top of the futon frame and then covered it in a sheet.

"Looks best kind," RJ remarked. He sat, bouncing.

"Hope you'll be comfortable." She fluffed a pillow, then pulled a quilt out of the large bag.

"It's as good a place as any to die," RJ replied.

"RJ!" Jean admonished.

"We're all going to die, Jean. The best we can hope for is to survive for a while."

"I don't want to think about it. Let's just get things ready for the crowd." Tears formed behind her eyes and she willed them to stay back. Now her house, normally her sanctuary, the place of peace and quiet, would be filled. She, who had reorganized her life to have a quiet spot in the middle of nowhere was trapped with a crowd. She'd cry later in her bedroom. But what else could she do? *Needs* must as her grandmother had always said.

RJ put the leaf in her table to make it big enough and it looked pretty good when it was done. Max brought over several kerosene lanterns and set them up, then left again.

"Do you wish you had stayed in Toronto given it seems the rest of the country is fine? The Americans came here because we're strategically located, and the federal government was too spineless to say no. It's all their fault, you know?" RJ grabbed another chair for the kitchen.

"Not just spineless. They wanted to be in on the action. Plus, the bases add to the economy, but it's how we became a target. Dollars always win. And no, I don't wish I'd stayed. I love it here."

"Wars take out military posts all the time. This attack was strategic," he said.

"Yes, and from what I'm hearing from the walkers, it seems the soldiers that survived are scattering all over, taking over, and setting up. Making those towns targets also." Jean nodded.

"They've been doing it for a while, even before the strike. The people have no choice but to take them in. They're armed soldiers." He set another chair down.

"The only reason they're not here is because we're an island. They can't land planes here. Can't move in their vehicles without running the ferry which is a lot of trouble. Best bet for us for now is to be as quiet as possible and let this all play out. Can you believe they've destroyed St. John's and Gander?" Her eyes welled up again.

"I'm trying not to think about it." RJ turned to look at Jean. "What's the point?"

"I can't help it. It's not all the time because I'm so busy trying to get things in order but every now and then somebody crosses my mind. A Facebook friend or somebody who used to live here who moved away." Jean's voice broke.

"I have convinced myself all the people I know are dead. I hope they are. It's easier."

"Easier? How is that easier? That's quite— callous."

RJ sat in a chair. She took one on the opposite side. He looked her straight in the eyes across the kitchen table. "Dead's better than maimed and suffering." He pushed his chair back as though the words had set the table fire and drew his cap down around his ears. "I'm going to go load up the sled, bring Lydia's bags up here, then I'll get some of Father's wood. We cut enough for a lifetime. It's all hidden away but all Father wants to do is cut wood. He'll be some happy he can cut it openly now!" He grinned.

"You'll bring Lydia and her granddaughter when you come back? How are you for fuel?" Jean realized he wasn't callous, that his reaction was protective of his own emotions. He wasn't uncaring, he was just handling it differently. Changing the subject. Perhaps his way was better.

"I'm good for Cleanfuel for now. I don't use much. The shop is low though, they didn't get their delivery before all this happened. Not that it matters, they've essentially shut down, keeping the stock for themselves. Can't say I blame them. They also kept all the ammunition. So, what we have on hand for hunting is all we have."

"That's Francis Richmond's doing, isn't it?" Jean stood, looked out the window. There seemed to be a division growing in the town between those who wanted to share and survive cooperatively and those who were battening down for the long haul in isolation.

"Oh yes, he's all over this." RJ's eyes narrowed.

"Well, I don't think there is anything we can do but do our best for everybody. It's early March. We have to figure out how to make do until spring. I think we can grow enough for everybody if everybody helps. I have a good stock of seeds and we will keep the potato eyes. Then, with fishing and hunting, we should be fine. But it'll be hard if we don't get help," Jean said.

"Francis thinks the Americans will come and save us all, bring us food. They're our allies so he doesn't think this will last. Idiot." RJ's laugh was mocking.

"The Americans? I doubt it. But we don't have a lot of choice, whatever happens." Jean rubbed the back of her hand over her forehead.

"It will, as I told him, make us a target if they do. I'd rather take my chances here like all our ancestors did, growing stuff, fishing, picking berries. I don't want to have to bow down to the Americans or the Russians. Or the Chinese. God knows who'll show up here. We don't know who's on our side anymore, who might be the enemy."

"I hadn't thought of the Russians or Chinese." Jean grew cold. There was no point in denying the possibility. Everything was possible. Yesterday there had been a capital city in this province, now it was obliterated.

"What about the Canadians? Perhaps our army or navy will come."

"I'm sure they'll show up eventually. They're here already I suppose, in some fashion. We must have officially entered the war now that we've been attacked. Nothing is impossible these days."

Impossible. The word hung in the kitchen. Yesterday that word comforted those who felt insulated here from the battles that had raged in other places these past months. It was impossible that the war would come here. Today the word was an invalid descriptor. Any narrative that contained it had been discredited by the exact events deemed to be preposterous less than twenty-four hours ago. It was *all* possible, including their own eradication.

"Or nobody comes, and we all live here happy ever after off the land," RJ said.

"That's our best-case scenario, so let's go with that while planning for the worst," Jean agreed, chewing her dry lip.

The door rattled. She jumped, expecting one of her new roommates to enter but instead it was Reg.

"I'd cook it all if I was you, it'll keep longer," the fire-chief, expert hunter, advised, handing her a large blue tub of seal meat, butchered into roasts, half dozen flippers set to one side.

"Yes, b'y!" RJ jumped up to help him get the tub to the sink. He'd offered to go but the truth was he didn't like sealing. He was glad that he didn't have to. But he liked the meat.

The water dripped as it did from all the taps. Moving water froze more slowly so without the furnace it was left to run. Frozen, broken pipes would be a disaster. It was bad enough they had no hot water. Jean already craved a shower but had to be satisfied with a sponge bath in her room later. The pump was plugged to the generator for now, Maggie having found another for her chickens, but fuel needed to be conserved so the less it was used the better.

She set about getting the large roaster. Reg declined her offer to stay for supper, his missus roasting a feed for their family and the new people occupying their two spare rooms. I'll bottle some tomorrow, she thought. Too much on the go to do it now. The house would be full soon. People would want to eat.

Lydia and her granddaughter, Ashlyn, showed up shortly after with a large grey female cat who spied Tom, hissed, and clamoured up on Lydia's shoulder.

The child's presence vanquished any negative talk. Making her happy and at home became their focus. Max arrived a while later, with a small bag and his pipe. He also brought over his old accordion. RJ picked up Jean's guitar and tuned it for her and they sang some old songs, drank a bit of rum and red wine, and whiled away the evening as though it were a campout. Even Lydia joined in, her once strong voice weakened by years of illness. For a time, the horror of their new reality was awash in a tiny shower of hope and song.

Until a new day dashed it away.

CHAPTER EIGHT

The sun has vanished, and the sky is a dingy grey. There are no stars at night. They're hidden by a fine ash that remains suspended in the air. I suspect it's radioactive. RJ thinks it's biological. Some people are sick. We're calling it the flu, but so far nobody who has it has recovered. They're staying ill, not getting worse, but not healing yet. Colin says there is nothing to be done. I hate keeping Ashlyn inside but—

The knock interrupted Jean's journaling. She'd kept one for years since a therapist recommended it, long before she ran away and found healing on Desolate Island. The note pads that recorded the boring details of her life, stacked in a blue bin in the attic, were now full of angst and drama again. This time, though, there was nowhere safe to run. Today's page was dated April 28, 2047.

She slapped the book shut, opened her bedroom door and RJ whispered, "May I come in, we need to talk."

She hesitated, then moved aside.

"More are sick," he said, perching at the edge of the bed, facing her when she sat back down, her back to her desk. "Colin is sure it's the dust that is making people sick. He's advised everybody to stay inside. Feels like the old pandemic shutdowns, but this time people can see the poison. So they are, wearing masks if they have to be outside but I don't know if it's working."

"I don't think it is. Lydia isn't well, and she hasn't been outside," Jean said.

"How are you feeling?"

"Fine, nothing. You?"

"Fit as a fiddle." He grinned.

"Maybe it is just the flu?"

RJ shook his head. "You know it's not. Colin is a nurse, he knows. He says you can survive radiation poisoning, but it depends on the amount of exposure. If that's what this even is. It's been really bad since the wind started blowing this way. This dust, whatever it is, causes the nausea to start and once it begins.... I also don't think we have any doubt the bombs were atomic at this point. There is also a rumour that some bio-bombs were also dropped in Deer Lake, but who knows what is real and what is rumour anymore?"

"Still no radio?"

"Not a blip from the outside world. Jean, that is what I want to discuss. I think we should leave here."

"Leave? How can we leave?"

"By boat. I have a boat."

"Where would we go? Where would we get Cleanfuel? The ice is still in, the ferry hasn't come back. We've used most of ours. "

"You know Dad, what he's like. He stowed away plenty of Cleanfuel. We have enough to get us across the gulf twice and we wouldn't go yet, we'd wait until late May. But I think we should think about it and plan for it."

"I feel safe here though. Nobody knows we're here or really cares, so why would we leave?"

"Because this place is sick. Whatever is in the air, it's poison."

"It still feels safer here. The wind will blow it all away once we get a good storm. And what if we get to Nova Scotia, then what? And who goes? All of us and your father? We leave the others?

"We'll work all that out, "RJ said. "And it doesn't feel safe here to me."

"We're here where we know what we have, who the people are. To leave and take a chance to go to what? It makes no sense. We don't even know what is out there."

"The rest of Canada is untouched so far as we can tell. And I don't see why anyone would attack them. Look, I've thought about this. The Americans were here because of our location, but the rest of Canada serves no purpose. Especially towards the north. While these idiots running the countries are lobbing bombs at each other, they still need to be strategic. Bombs cost money. I would imagine the US is a disaster, as is much of Europe and we know the Middle East is a crater. But Northern Canada, it's on its own, barren, sparsely populated, nobody wants it, it's forgotten. It's the best place to be. To survive. It won't have radiation. But even Nova Scotia, New Brunswick, or Quebec are safer than here. They never got hit in the last world wars. Newfoundland always has. Anyway, so you know, when the ice breaks up, I'm taking my chances and going up and through the straights and making my way across to Quebec."

"Your boat isn't very big."

"It's big enough. If we rigged out the hold for people, we could take our own people. And the ones at Dad's house too. Even the ones next door at Max's place. I can navigate. Dad's good too but he's not well. Your skills would be helpful. Think about it. I think we're closer to the front lines here. On them even. Plus, with everybody getting sick, it's only a matter of time before— " His eyes cast down, she knew the last bit. *Before they died.*

"What about the rest of the town?"

"They're not our responsibility. Look, do what you want okay, but I'm going. Can we keep this conversation between us though? I'm getting stuff ready, and I haven't told Dad yet. Maybe I'll just pretend we're going off sealing when the time comes. I don't know. I need to think about it more myself."

She nodded and he could see her movement by the light of the flickering candle.

After he left, Jean considered what he had said. Leave. Vamoose. It had been her strongest instinct the day she had bought this house after a twelve-hour visit. Back then she had fled here for sanctuary. She never wanted to leave but she sure as hell wanted to survive for a few more years too. God, she hated governments and their trigger-happy leaders. Out here, alone, they'd caused no harm to anybody, yet were affected by power hungry, greedy, selfish, war-mongering—

A low, distant thunder-like rumble interrupted her internal rant.

"What the hell is that?" RJ asked, throwing open the door before she could interpret what she was hearing. "Let's go, blow out the damned candle."

They had a strict no lights at night policy in place in the community. Some people had darkened their windows with blankets, but had nothing to light their homes with anyway, and turned in at dark and woke at dawn. Jean always lit tea light candles off the stove flame and took them to her bedroom at night. Her windows were blackened by the heavy curtains she'd installed when she had moved to the house, the bright sun waking her earlier than she liked. Now she rarely threw them open, the outside so dreary and depressing, the dirt-grey snow a reminder of the horror of the war nearby.

She blew at the flame and followed RJ. Max, Lydia, and Ashlyn met them in the kitchen.

"Stay here, keep it dark," RJ instructed.

Ashlyn sobbed and said, "Mommy." Lydia coughed and pulled her close.

Jean touched the little girl's shoulder. She tried to reassure them as the rumbling grew closer. "It'll be fine, we'll go see, okay?"

Coats on and hats in place, RJ and Jean went out. Max's house remained blackened, but the door opened, and Marilyn, their new neighbour, looked out. RJ shouted, "Go back in!" but his voice was muffled by the rumbling. They must have understood his motion, however, as she ducked back inside.

The roar grew louder. Jean trembled like the earth around her as whatever it was closed in on them. She covered her ears, looked skyward, then lifted her left hand like a visor at her forehead. She reached for RJ's right hand as the air around her shuddered. It approached from the east, but it was difficult to gauge how close it was. Being out in the open, in the centre of the garden, was counterintuitive but Jean remained although every inch of her screamed run and hide. RJ and Jean circled around. Looking upwards, holding hands, trying to see what was about to hit them.

The belly of it, flat and low, was but a shade lighter than the night. It propelled forward over their heads and Jean grabbed RJ in an embrace, the instinct for human contact in her last moments, overwhelming. He wrapped his arms around her and held on. Wing lights blinked like falling stars as they stood, transfixed, staring up at the fuselage of the giant warplane, expecting something to drop from its belly at any moment.

"If I'm going to die," RJ said directly into her ear. Then he tipped her head back and kissed her, his lips warming hers as the large aircraft passed over head. A winding sound filled the night and the ground shook.

"RJ," she said when he let her go. The plane drowned out her voice.

He pulled away, looked up, his eyes following the large plane until it vanished from sight.

"Let's go in and tell the others it was nothing."

Jean walked ahead of him. Relieved, shaken, disturbed. It was hardly *nothing*.

"Just surveillance, I'd guess," RJ said once inside.

Jean reassured everybody that's all it was too, although they didn't know for sure. If they were being surveilled they had no idea who was watching them or why. She sent them all to their rooms. Jean gave little Ashlyn a kiss on the top of her head and RJ ruffled her soft hair.

RJ followed Jean into her room. Good. She needed to talk to him. He closed the door behind them. She turned to him in the blackness, then reached out and touched him. He pulled her close, picked up where they left off, desperate and hungry for touch, for escape, for human comfort. She moved them towards the bed, words secondary to the comfort and desire she needed in that moment.

If I'm going to die, she thought.

Afterwards, they clung to each other, as if it were the beginning, not the conclusion of lovemaking. They heated each other's bodies with hands that roamed and moved slower until finally, they relaxed into stillness.

RJ settled in, holding Jean close. He adjusted a pillow

until they were both comfortable. He stroked her hair then kissed the top of her head.

Then he whispered to her, his voice barely audible. "Jean."

"Yes?" she responded, holding her breath. Waiting for the words that might explain why they were here, like this suddenly.

"Your fuckin' futon is hard as a rock," RJ whispered.

She guffawed, an unfamiliar, and eager sound. She covered her mouth, stifling her laughter unable to stop her shoulders from heaving and tears from forming in her eyes. RJ caught the wave and fell into hysterical giggles with her.

"Shhhh," she whispered before more peels of laughter rang out. She muffled it with the blanket.

"It's not—even fun— funny," she said when she caught her breath. The hilarity was more from the unexpectedness of his words than the content.

Joy, once a daily part of her life, had been absent for too long. This was the first time she'd laughed out loud since the power went out. She decided she'd do more of it. Goddamn it. If this was the close of her life, she would spend it being as happy as she could be, for as long as she had.

She laid a palm on RJ's chest, felt the pound of his heart, and smiled.

CHAPTER NINE

Jean, a planner, had enough cat food, dry and canned, to last one cat at least a year. Tom didn't seem bothered about having to share with Princess. They ate at proximity, then curled together, grooming each other as though old friends reunited. Perhaps they were. Both had been outdoor felines with a safe island to roam. Maybe along some dark path, on a starry nocturnal walk, they'd encountered each other before.

By contrast, Lydia's lack of appetite depleted her energy and he weight loss was stark. She suffered significant pain as well, having run out of her regular arthritis medication. Her wrists were swollen, her knees ached, and the sheets hurt on her body. The bed was still more comfortable than being up, so she stayed there, sheets and all, suffering through.

Ashlyn, the three-year old, had big, grey, solemn, soul-grabbing eyes. "It's because she's been here before," Lydia had said, to explain what she described as Ashlyn's *old soul*. Jean didn't go for much of that new-wave hokey but sometimes when Ashlyn spoke, her wisdom great in a tiny body, she almost did.

Jean and RJ now undertook to preserve everything they could in mason jars, including the extra seal and the moose that might soften in the freezer. Many of the jars were Lydia's contribution, several dozens of them along with seals and lids. She had been one of twelve and their collection of jars was for a large family too many for her on her own. She'd not been able to preserve due to her disability recently anyway, so they sat dusty on shelves for years. She felt good that she could contribute, given her illness had her feeling like a burden to the others.

The counter was always *lined off*, as Max put it. They had food. They had wood. They had water. They could live for a while off what they had. Many were not so fortunate. Gunshots rang out frequently as seals and birds were harvested.

"Cat's cradle, RJ?" Ashlyn's speech was perfect, no child-like lisp, no mispronunciations of the r sound. Young, but mature.

"You bet, pretty face," he said.

"Can we play Go Fish again tonight? she asked.

"Yes, my lady, but let's do this first." RJ pulled the string from his pocket, his face interested in her, no pretense, loving the interaction.

Their fingers met through the game. His tucked through the string, pinched it in exactly the right place, twisted his wrist so that now the tiny pattern was on the tips of his fingers. Ashlyn thought for a moment before she crossed her wrists and used her pinky fingers to do the next step so that it inverted, a perfect cradle onto her tiny hands.

So, it went in the room. His low laughter, her delighted squeals, the rattle as Jean washed dishes and Max dried, the dishwasher useless except as a drain board. Mason jars dried upside down in it, prepared for the next round of bottling.

"Mommy's going to die, isn't she?" Ashlyn's hands had just been freed from the cat's cradle and RJ, trapped by the fingertips, was forced to look into her eyes and answer. Jean moved behind her, standing close.

"We don't know that," RJ said.

But they did. Colin said the sick appeared to be incurable. Many were bedridden, weakening daily. Lydia was the worse case.

"She will." The little girl nodded. "The air is poisoned by the dust. I can taste the poison on it when I breathe outdoors. Can't you taste it? It's like when you lick a cold spoon with no ice cream. Can we ever have ice cream again? Or is there no ice cream when there is a war?" Ashlyn's voice was a small, pristine sound in a room of crackling wood and purring cats.

"Ashlyn, your grandmother, uh, mommy, may die. It might be the poison air, but it might be the flu. We're not all sick. You're not sick at all."

Ashlyn nodded. "I know that three-year-olds can die, but I don't want to die when I'm three. I want to be a big girl someday. I want to have babies. Why don't you have babies, Jean?"

"I never got married, never found anyone to have a family with. Some people aren't meant to be parents, I'm one of them," Jean replied.

"Like my honest-to-God mom? She was a broken parent, Mommy says. If Mommy dies, I won't have any parents. I will be an orphan. Is that right?"

"Are you worried about being cared for, sweetheart? When your mom dies?" RJ asked. Softening the words was pointless, he thought. This child knew too damned much.

The child bobbed her head, her big eyes filling with

tears to have her fears spoken so accurately.

"We will always take care of you, Ashlyn," Jean said.

"Me and Jean will, promise," RJ agreed.

"And Princess?"

"Tom will take care of Princess," Jean said, looking over at the two, sprawled together in front of the wood stove, bellies filled with seal offal to save on the tinned stock.

"It's good that we all take care of each other when things are bad," Ashlyn replied. "I think if we take care of each other then everything else will take care of itself. And if we all end up dying, well we were going to anyway, sometime. But I do want to be four someday but if I can't at least I'd love to see summer again one more time. It's all too grey now. The sun brings rainbows. And butterflies. I like to run with the butterflies. I don't chase them, that scares them. We just run together. I miss rainbows and summer."

The door to Max's room closed with a thunk. The possibility of not having another summer for a three-year-old, to one who had seen over eighty of them, was a bit much for the old guy.

Ashlyn slipped off her chair and laid on her belly on the hearth with the two cats, petting them both as they purred under her ministrations. There, little legs kicked the air in fluffy socks and whispered sweet words aimed at two contented cats. "Get out and catch mice and birds and rats to save your cat food. You can't buy stuff anymore."

RJ's eyes met Jean's. She shook her head, a small movement, barely noticeable.

He motioned for her to come sit with him on the futon that had been returned to the kitchen now that his nights were spent in her bed.

"She's quite the kid. Sage, you know?" he remarked, his voice a whisper.

"Yeah, to see summer again. Such a simple wish. I want to see summer again too." Jean leaned into him, an ache behind her eyes. His arm came across her shoulders, kneading the muscles in her arm beneath the cables of the big sweater she'd completed a few days prior.

"What happened to little girls wishing for Barbie dolls, RJ?"

"Powerful old men decided they should wish for summer instead."

"We can't even promise her that."

"I won't make promises, but I'm going to try to make sure she sees a fourth birthday. There *is* news." His eyes never left the child.

"Tell me." She knew from his voice that she didn't want to know.

"It's been confirmed. The US is in bad shape. The White House, Capital Building, and The Pentagon are all gone."

Jean sat upright. "Where did you hear that?" She glanced at Ashlynn who was still immersed in her song to the cats.

"Radio came in again for a while. Reg told me when I was out getting turrs. I threw the birds back by the way. I think there was something wrong with them. They were right inside the bay. Turrs don't come in here. Anyway, the president is gone, the entire congress, pretty much all of DC is wiped out."

"Jesus wept. But I'm not sure I'm sad. That president, that congress, this is all on them. Perhaps now things will get better. Christ, we need more batteries for the radio.

I'm the mayor, I should have a way to listen for this news. I suppose I am. No, I'm not anymore. There is no mayor, no structure. We're each on our own. What was in place before means nothing now. We are in a new time."

"I think you're right. Anyway, the bombs have stopped for now, they said. I don't know if they've run out or if the people ordering them dropped blew themselves up. The rest of Canada is fine, though we can't hear of anything more than references to the bombing in Newfoundland because the radio signal is from somewhere on the American eastern seaboard. They don't say their exact location. Guess they're afraid to."

"You still plan to leave when it gets decent outside? If the bombs have stopped, then we won't be targets even if the Americans come."

"We can't be sure, and I don't want to be here. I want to find a place where it's a bit normal, where there are a lot of people, perhaps where there is work. So yeah, I'm still going. Are you coming with me?"

"I think I am, but let's wait until Lydia—" She let the words trail off.

"She'll be gone by the time the ice moves off."

"I think she could be gone by tomorrow."

They both looked at Ashlyn. They'd committed to her these past few weeks even if they'd just told her now. She needed security and they were it. It was a daunting idea, raising a child but that's what it appeared they'd be doing when Lydia succumbed to her illness. At least currently the focus was simple. Their only responsibility for the foreseeable future was keeping her alive.

CHAPTER TEN

The ocean opened up in late April, the ice driven off the land by the seas and tides with the remnants of the floes tucked upon beaches in coves around the islands. The snow remained, banked high, the grey dingy dust covered now in two feet of new, heavier banks. The temperatures stayed low, and spring battled to arrive.

One fine day RJ, Reg, and a couple of other locals took a small boat and headed over to the ferry dock. There they found the *MV Captillan II* bobbing like a ghost ship, eerie after being abandoned and now possibly unsound. Her ramp was down, and the power was out. The door to the terminal banged against the side of the wall, its tap-tap-tap an annoying rhythm in the still air. The vacant parking lot had the men wondering what the crew found when they ended up wherever they had headed when they abandoned their worksite.

The men siphoned Cleanfuel from her tanks, filling the jerry cans they had brought and any other containers they discovered on board, and packed up all that they could, becoming looters out of necessity.

"I think they headed home," RJ said.

"That's what I would do." Reg lugged a bucket of fuel to the edge of the ramp and set it down.

"Look at that." RJ pointed along the shoreline, the tide low, the beach near the dock exposed. "What are they?"

Gulls?" Reg replied. There were a dozen or so lying dead on the ice-lined beach, decomposition a slow rot in the cold water.

"Still live gulls down our way," RJ noted, catching up, kicking one over. "There were always lots of shags around this cove, even since the change." He eyed the open waters of the bay that sheltered the dock, looking for cormorants that usually flew, often in pairs, low over the surface. Not one of the sleek black birds shot across the water.

"'Tis frightening," Reg said. He watched the other two men, Jack and Layden, load up the boat with blankets.

RJ's hands played with some batteries he'd stuffed into his pockets.

"Canary in the coal mine?" Reg asked, referring to the dead and disappearing birds.

"I think so," RJ replied. "Never had cormorants down our way but used to be maggoty with them here."

"We got ducks too, been eating them like crazy. Might be poison," Reg said.

"Why do you think some is sick and not others, Reg?" Layden Fancey asked, walking in on the conversation. "Birds dead here, but not back home?"

"Nurse says some are more acceptable to it." Reg drew a smoke out of a case and lit it, then pulled down his mask and drew hard on it.

Reg's malapropism brought a grin to RJ's face. "That's right, those who are weakest. Lydia had influenza and pneumonia right after Christmas. Plus, the arthritis. She was not well to start. As for the birds. Poison thicker here perhaps?"

"Perhaps. Lydia's hanging on though?"

"By a thread, b'y."

"You and Jean is a couple now I hear." Layden Fancey wasn't known for tact. The others appreciated it because they were all wondering.

"Got to love a small town and its gossip. Jean is a good woman and what odds about it?" RJ grinned but his eyes held a challenge.

"No odds about it, proper t'ing, I says." Reg gave RJ a thump on the shoulder. Sparks flew out of his cigarette and drifted down to the rocks.

"Good looking woman, b'y. No odds is right," Layden agreed. His missus would enjoy the confirmation of the gossip, he thought.

Their small boat sat low in the water under the weight of supplies. The men had divided it equally. There was more, and they would come back and forth across the run with containers to refill over time.

Cleanfuel was the most precious. Many were not running the generators now because they had so little of it and the Babcocks who ran the store were out as well. Those with solar were okay, but here things lagged and most had not invested in it back in the thirties when they weren't sure the town would make it. But the town had survived, as it had the Great Intermission back in the early twenties when a series of pandemics and their ensuing depression had nearly ended things. Then they tapped into A-zon technology jobs, and everybody became employed. There was something about Desolate and its people who had always found a way to make it through. *So far.*

They would share their findings with some of their neighbours. Not Francis Richmond though, tight old geezer. He had plenty, his generated electric lights taunted every other resident of the small town who lived by candle and lantern. He wouldn't get a drop when he ran out. And he would eventually. They all would.

After their return, RJ maneuvered the small boat to align beside the larger longliner *June Delight*. Named after his mother, he shared ownership of the vessel with his father. She was an older boat, but they still owed money on her. He had no way of knowing if the bank still automatically withdrew the payments. He tethered to the larger boat and boarded her.

The *June* fired up easily for him. Too big for one person to handle, Reg showed up shortly after to give him a hand. Soon, speed boat in tow, he pulled off and headed to Jean's dock.

Jean watched from the kitchen window. The longliner, large against her small wharf, pulled in. Max met them, caught the painter, and secured it. She hadn't ever docked anything besides her small eighteen-foot outboard that now lay, bottom up, on the slipway. Somehow the big boat fit though, and ropes and moorings soon secured The *June Delight* fast against the rock-filled frame of her dock, with its planked platform.

A speck in the distance caught June's eye as she turned away. She pivoted back and gasped. She picked up the binoculars and adjusted them, zooming in on the large grey form. A ship, long and thin, bearing an American flag that fluttered in the cold April breeze posed against the horizon. The bow was pointed in their direction. She watched a bit longer and determined that it was anchored. It had not been there in the morning when she glided the binoculars over the waters, checking for the men who had gone off to the other side to see if the ferry would ever run again. But it was there now, a large grey streak against the horizon.

She placed the binoculars back on the counter, unable to leave the three-year old alone sleeping on the futon to go tell the men.

Worried about Ashlyn, she went over and stroked her forehead. No fever. *She is tired*, Jean told herself. She stayed up too late playing Slap Jack with RJ. Jean curled her lip to one side. Lydia, her body as hot as the kitchen stove, now lay unconscious. Jean couldn't bear the thought of the child getting sick too.

Max was next door. The inhabitants of his house, Dave and Marilyn Collins and their son Matt, had run low on a few things. He dropped off some bottled meat and salt cod and made a trip to the cellar to bring them vegetables. The family was quiet and grateful and never asked, but Jean shared her supplies nonetheless. Having Max come to them had been meant to conserve supplies, but the new family had blown that plan to bits. To help out, they sawed and stacked wood, came to help out with whatever was needed, and Marilyn took Ashlyn sometimes, her boy Matt only a couple of years older. They'd nicknamed the family The Maxes and taken to calling the family at RJ's dad's place The Ralphs. Both families loved the light-hearted titles, appreciating the sacrifice that both Max and the two real Ralphs had made for them.

RJ and Reg stomped into the kitchen a short while later.

"There's a ship outside the run," Jean said, nodding to the binoculars.

RJ held them up and looked. "US Navy. Battleship, I suppose. I don't know, could be a supply ship or a tanker, but looks to be an amphibious assault ship to me." RJ handed them to Reg.

" Amphibi...what?" Reg asked, after a look, hand already on the doorknob, having seen enough and wanting to tell his family about it.

"A ship that can come ashore or drop soldiers ashore to go to war."

"Best kind then," he said. "I'll see you after." He closed the door behind him.

"That's terrifying." Jean looked out the window again.

"Everything is terrifying these days. I knew they were out there, patrolling. Had to be. They're supposed to be allies, but I don't know if I trust that they are."

"Does that make it safe to leave? Or is that more dangerous?"

"Odds are they're not looking to engage with tiny fishing boats."

"Do you think there are any of our ships around?" The idea of a Canadian ship comforted her.

"I don't know. The Americans have upwards of five hundred naval ships, at least they did before the war. We have maybe—forty? I think fewer. Odds are if the Americans are here, then we don't need one of ours. They would have spread out. Oh, I got you something."

He dropped batteries on the table. Jean grabbed one that rolled. There were different sizes. He pulled more out of another pocket, and she caught them as well. Her eyes lit up at the batteries like they would have at a gift of flowers.

"Oh, RJ, this is awful." Jean stared at the batteries, mind on the ship.

"What? You don't like batteries?" He grinned. "The ferry crew took to the woods, maid. They don't need them." He glanced out the window.

"Shut up. Yes, thank you for the batteries, but I mean

about the Americans. Should we call a meeting? Tell people about the ferry? The navy ship? Maybe start a regular watch off the lookout? Rotate people?"

"Yes. I think we should, Jean. What do we do about Ashlyn?" He nodded his head.

"Go see if Marilyn will come. She can bring Matt, watch Ashlyn, and tend to Lydia. We'll fill her in after we come back."

"Lydia will go tonight," he whispered, glancing at the child.

"Yes, I think so. Maybe we should bring Colin back to nurse her. I don't want to be the one—"

"Good idea. You get ready here, I'll go ask Marilyn to come over, then I'll head down to ring the bell. Hide those batteries."

The door closed behind him with a woof of cold. The temperatures hit the pluses most days now, spring pushing its way through the air with a warm, constant breeze denting the last of the drifts that lay against fences, diminishing them.

The usual relief that accompanied the signs of the hopeful season was absent this year. The poison still lingered, if invisible. Most of those who originally took sick were determined to be past the point of recovery. Thin bodies sipped bland soup and water through reused straws. There was no medicine for the malady even if they knew for sure what it was. More became ill daily. It was the second wave of sickness that set Jean's mind about leaving.

Everything they needed to survive for several more months might be here, but clean air was more important and necessary. They decided to invite the neighbours to go with them but closer to the time. They told no one, not even Max, of the plan. He'd be invited of course. Until then, Jean needed to maintain the image of being mayor. It was a meaningless title, but people seemed to look to her, and it gave her purpose.

Marilyn arrived with Matt, and Jean slipped on her coat and boots, meeting Max on the crook of the road. She tucked her arm in his. The bell tolled when they were halfway between the school and their garden, a slow bong-bing, bong-bing followed by a pause. Not an emergency but important.

Jean and Max quickened their steps. It all felt like an emergency to them.

CHAPTER ELEVEN

The bell tolled until it appeared all that were coming had arrived. Jean waited at the top of the stage, RJ at her side, and Reg on one end along with Layden Fancey. People poured in, strain on their faces, fear in their eyes. But there was some laughter too, the humour of a given moment always bigger than its horror, if a laugh could be found.

Francis and Mallory Richmond sat in the front row, defiance on his face, defeat on hers. Jean suspected there would be trouble today and her hand shook.

They could not justify using the Cleanfuel for the generator and the high windows let in enough light anyway. Wrapped in their jackets, the people waited. As a sign that spring approached, some had their hats off and hoods down.

RJ's sharp whistle silenced the throng. Jean thanked him before speaking.

"We've got an American war ship off from the cove, quite far away yet. It appears to be anchored but the bow is pointed this way. We thought everybody should be informed that we may have visitors at some point."

Dust motes floated in the sunbeams amidst the silence that lasted as they absorbed this new information.

Francis Richmond's voice cracked the quiet like an axe on a block. "We're saved! The Americans have saved us! They'll have supplies and fuel. Medicine for the sick. Perhaps they'll be able to tell us when the power will come back, and the internet too. They're probably repairing everything by this time. This is good news!"

"I'm not so sure it's quite like that." Jean kept her voice calm. "The attacks were aimed at the American bases. If they're here in Desolate, we're not invisible anymore. We can't stop them from coming, but I think we should be aware that having Americans here doesn't mean we'll be safer. We'd more likely become a military target."

"Why the hell are you being so negative?" Francis shot back. "These are the Americans, *allies*. Of course they're here to help. They're probably winning the war by now and fixing it all up."

"She's not being negative, Francis, she's being realistic," RJ said.

"Oh, boyfriend sticking up for you now is he, Mayor?" Francis responded.

"Did you really just say that, Francis? Did you just insinuate there is something wrong with two consenting adults having a personal relationship? In Goddamned 2047? Are you also actually asking if I need somebody to stick up for me? Because if you think that, you are sorely mistaken. All you've done since we've been in this situation is be negative. While we've been trying to get everybody through this, you've been holed up in your B&B waiting for fucking tourists. It's the end of the world out there, half of us have radiation poisoning or some other Jeezley sickness and you're worried about the friggin' Wi-Fi?"

"Who made you king?" Francis stepped forward, his

rotund body drawn upright, fists clenched at the sides. His tiny wife, Mallory, grabbed his arm, but he threw her off with a swat. She stumbled backwards, her chair tipping so that she wound upon the floor. Several people around her moved forward to assist and Francis raised his fists, threatening them, sweat beading on his ruddy face despite the cool air. He grabbed Mallory by the arm, stood her upright and pointed a finger in her face. "Sit or I will sit you," he ordered.

RJ leapt from the stage, pulled Francis around by the shoulder and brought a fist to his face where it connected with a loud crack. The hefty man dropped. The audience let out a coordinated gasp.

"Yes!" The shout came from the crowd as Reg and Layton rushed forward.

Francis tried to get back up, hand over his jaw but couldn't. Mallory shook herself off, embarrassed. Jean met her eyes, then went down to her and reached out her hand. She hesitated a moment before taking it. Jean led her away while RJ stood over Francis, fist still raised. The crowd pushed forward, hoping for more. Several of the women followed Jean and Mallory outside.

"Can you walk up with RJ, if I don't come back?" she asked Max, who nodded, glancing at Mallory.

"You can come to my place, Mallory, stay with me if you want to get away. Would you like to stay with me?" Jean offered.

"I don't know, he's crazy. He might come up after me." Mallory whispered. Her eyes filled, the kindness too much. She'd endured so much these past months, the anger of the situation escalating her husband's violence.

"Get on the Quad," Claire of the Anglican women's group ordered. "I'll take you to get your stuff. You are going to Jean's and that's that."

Jean nodded. Everyone always suspected Mallory's situation. With the assault in the hall, there was proof of physical abuse and nobody needed to tolerate that these days.

"RJ is staying at my place. He'll keep him away. You don't have to go back. Promise," Jean reassured her.

Claire and Mallory went off on the electric all-terrain vehicle and Jean went inside. She nudged Max's arm, so he'd know she was back after all.

He winked. "You got some man there."

Jean snorted a laugh. "Not too shabby, I must say."

"Nope." Max laughed back, partly because she sounded just like a local.

"Where's my wife?" Francis demanded, his eyes black with rage.

"Claire is taking her home." Jean moved towards the stage.

"Don't even blink until Jean finishes up this meeting, arse," RJ threatened, hand on Francis' chest. "You won't like your new smile if you do."

Jean made her way to the podium and the crowd settled back, listening.

"Alright, that was exciting and wholly unnecessary. I do want to say, I'm not in charge here. I am only trying to offer guidance. You all can do as you please, but we've always been a community that helps each other out and we helped all who came over across the ice too. I've shared my stores to whoever needed what I had, and I will continue to do so. But the reality is that things are never going to be what they were."

"You listen to the mayor," Roy Pearcey, the church lay reader said. Jean also suspected he was the voice of the

"Yes!" expressed at RJ's blow to Francis's face. He hopped up on stage. His beagle Rufus followed him. "We have always been a close-knit town, and we always come together in times of trouble. Jean has not misled us yet. We must stay with one another, be strong, fortify against the temptation to go it alone."

Roy scanned the crowd. So many missing, too sick to attend. He had been watching the community, trying to sort what precisely was happening. It appeared, out of all the crowd, Jean's people had the best chance of survival. He was smart enough to align with them for that reason. Though he'd been quiet these past months, now he decided it was wise to step up and be heard.

"Let's support Jean's leadership, it hasn't failed us yet."

"The gulls are dead at the ferry wharf," Layden said, walking up the steps and on to the stage. Roy stepped back.

"What does that mean?" Sarah Pomeroy, the town clerk asked.

Somebody coughed. Layden waited until the hacking subsided. Several people patted the woman who struggled to stop so that she wouldn't delay the answer.

"The birds is dying," he said. "The poison, radiation, whatever it is, it's deadly. The gulls here around the island are alive so far, but we're not so far away from the dock. Possibly the ones we saw washed in on the tide from far away, but we can't possibly think they could drop a bomb on the other side of the province, and nothing would get to us here. You all saw that dust."

"Are we all going to die?" Maggie Rogers asked. Several sobs came from those around her, and one man left the room. The rest were quiet and somber. Waiting.

"We don't know. But I think some of us are," Jean said. She glanced at RJ who nodded approval.

"We need to get out of here," Layden said.

"And go where?" Mildred Marche asked from the second row.

"We could take the longliners across the gulf, or go up to Labrador, or over to Quebec," he suggested. His eyes darted around the room, wondering if anyone would be interested in going.

"Is there enough fuel for that?" Maggie asked.

"Francis got lots, we got what was on the ferry and the shop might have some. If we figured it all out, I think so."

"Babcocks at the shop, they're out. All of them are sick too."

"That's too bad. Well, we could load up two or three and make our way across. Fix up the holds, make room."

RJ looked at Jean, and with a slight shake of his head suggested she not share their own thoughts and plans."

Look," she said. "If you all want to leave, nothing can stop you. But we're a community and right now we're all here and we're together. I have some batteries for the radio so I'm going to keep it on and listen for news."

"Maybe we could call the ship from the boat radios," Reg suggested. He'd never trusted mobile phone service at sea. Few of the men here did. So, he still had an old two-way radio.

"That's a proper good idea," Max said.

"I think it is too, thanks, Reg. We'll work on doing that and figuring out what to say if we do contact them. I think we have to be careful."

Max piped up, "I think we should take watch from the lookout. Two by two, four-hour shifts. Who wants to volunteer?"

Nearly every hand in the room went up and Jean laughed.

"I know how you feel," she said. "I think we all want to be useful. Please come to the house with ideas. I'm the mayor even if not everybody thinks I am, and I do think we need a home base. I'll be it until we don't need it anymore if you like."

Francis made to get up and RJ shook his head no, so he sat again. Jean shook hers no, too, confirming that they needed more time to get Mallory out of the Inn and to her place.

The crowd shoved forward, somebody had a pen and paper, and they made a schedule for watch. Tallboy Lookout was the highest point of land and from there the entire surrounding sea could be viewed. It had a shelter made of rocks lifted up over the twenty-minute grade by ancestors. It was a great place to watch the navy ship and report back. Having two people meant the time went faster and one could watch while the other reported if there was movement.

Finally, it was just the three of them walking home together under a black velvet and rhinestone sky.

"We is leaving, iddin we?" Max asked, as they crested the hill, his dialect as old as this settlement that had brought his ancestors from Europe.

"We'll see," Jean allowed.

"I had the old two-way radio going today. I didn't hear a sound. I suppose different frequencies, or they have all the new technologies, but if there is any way I want to talk to the Americans too," RJ said.

"Let's go home. We have another person living with us now if she wants to stay. The futon will have to go to the living room again. Let's see what kind of drama we're dealing with. Francis is going to lose his mind when he realizes Mallory isn't there. We have to get home before he does," Jean said.

Max started into a little jog, his arms bent like wings.

"Slow down, old man," RJ said, laughing.

"Jeez, you two, like having a punt in tow, draggin' me back." Max shortened his stride to match theirs, fake grumbling about slow youngsters.

They all laughed and walked home together to the point.

CHAPTER TWELVE

Mallory came to stay. Once the futon was in place, she asked to sleep. "I've not slept well in a long time," she said. "I never knew when he would—"

"I understand. And now, with these latest events, the war I mean, it's worse?"

"Yeah, way worse." She lowered her eyes, the warm wash of shame in their depths. Jean reached out and pulled her into a hug and Mallory collapsed into her shoulders and sobbed. After some time, she lifted her head and wiped her eyes.

"Relief," she explained. She desperately needed a good night's sleep without the possibility of a night rage, a pacing angry man claiming that his freedoms were being hampered, that there really was no war and it was all made up to make him suffer. And then there was the volley of punches that would land against her thin body and leave her crying on the floor, too wounded to care if she lived or died. She wiped her eyes, hoping that the gratitude she felt for their kindness showed. She didn't have the words, not yet. But they would come.

"Get some rest," Jean advised and Mallory left to do just that, shutting the door behind her carefully.

Jean went into the other room and tucked Ashlyn in.

Lydia's ragged breath rattled in the other bed. Every day Jean was surprised that her chest rose and her heart, beat, clinging to a life already lost to the ages. Ashlyn slept on a made-up mattress on the floor at the bottom of Lydia's bed, refusing to leave knowing that one day she would be gone forever. Until then the child insisted on sleeping near the grandmother who had rescued her when she was too young to remember. "Goodnight, butterfly," Jean said to the child, closing the door behind her.

RJ and Max both turned in early too after a nip at the rum and a rehashing of the fight, being far more celebratory than the situation warranted. But they needed release and so Jean let them revel in the joy of seeing Francis flop to the floor when RJ decked him. Plus, Jean too thought Francis deserved the punch, but not as much as Mallory deserved her deliverance from his abuse.

That left Claire, who'd brought Mallory up, and Jean, alone in the kitchen. They sipped weak tea, by lamplight.

Claire lowered her voice and glanced at the door behind which Mallory slept.

"She's bruised all over, not on her face but everywhere else. She tried to hide it, but I saw."

"Jesus. We always knew, I suppose. With all the laws now, you wouldn't think. I mean intimate partner abuse is an automatic jail term these days, followed by intense therapy. But out here, isolated with no police he could get away with it. Probably why he came here. I feel bad. I just thought she was a stuck-up snob and I should have known."

"Me too. And she's so thin, just skin over bones. But not sick like Lydia. They're almost out of food, you know? He was holding out, barely feeding her anything. That said, they don't have much that is useful anyway. Oddly they did have a lot of flour. I took two twenty-five-pound bags, one for me and one for you. He got it on sale a couple years ago, Mallory said. Don't seem spoiled or anything."

"Really? We thought he would have stock. Being a business and all."

"He didn't, nope. He has a lot of Cleanfuel. Bought it when prices were low, before the rations and stocked up. But they were not doing well, their line of credit and credit cards maxed-out so they didn't have much on hand. They tried to get stuff from the Babcocks at the shop, but they're not selling. Not that the hoarding helped, they've all got the nuclear flu too." Claire sipped her tea and sighed.

"We're getting low on ammunition," Jean said. "The cellar is getting low too but we're still alright for food. For now."

"We're pretty tight too at our place," Claire replied. "We eat lots of meat and bottled carrots. It's boring but better than starving."

"Yeah, not sure how long we can last on this island. If the birds die off, might be others that do too, the fish, the lobster."

"Gord wants to leave. Take the longliner and go west, get to Canada."

"Still rough water for that." Jean wondered if she should mention that RJ had the same idea but decided to keep quiet. Maybe they should all leave as a community, load up the boats and cross towards the other side as a convoy.

"Well, I best get home, doing the wash tomorrow." Claire pushed herself up. Her sweater hung from her frame. Jean looked closely at her. Her face, fully made up, had thinned over the past month.

"That is something I miss, the laundry machines. Here, take some bottles of meat," Jean insisted. She opened a cupboard and removed a few jars.

"Oh my, is that seal? I could never turn down seal. Never learned how to bottle myself. Never needed to. Thank you."

"Seal, rabbit, and moose. You got jam?" She slipped the jars into a cloth bag.

"No, I make it fresh, so I have none left. I love it on fried dough, thanks! Got any yeast? Don't suppose you have. Been making flat dough for a while and I'm a bit tired of it."

"Yes, here's a few sleeves. Okay, good. You need anything else let me know. Other than teabags. I can't believe I'm low on teabags."

Jean walked Claire to the door, locked it, then made her way to the bedroom. Her bones ached with the weight of a life interrupted and the heaviness of the pain the others suffered too. She climbed between the sheets. They had a slight odour. She missed having crisp sheets and clean pillowcases on a regular basis, but laundry was spared along. The washer could no longer be used, the generator set aside for real emergencies. Hand washing it was a pain, and they could only dry in certain weather outside. Anyway, if tomorrow was good, she'd do these sheets. She moved against the warmth of RJ, too tired to care. She touched his back, feeling the hardness of his muscles underneath his warm skin. She moved closer, then yawned once before falling into a slumber that lasted for nearly ten hours.

CHAPTER THIRTEEN

The sheets flapped in the wind, two days after Mallory arrived, the cool and sunny day the first opportunity to blow them dry.

God, but standards had changed, Jean thought. Clothing was worn over and over, and hand washed using an old scrub board that had adorned her wall as an antique, revived to allow for agitation. Jean had washed the sheets then RJ's strong hands had wrung excess water back into the sink, with a twist. Then he rolled them in towels to dry them further. She had battled the westerly winds that blew them high into the air, flipping and flapping as she pinned them fast. She followed them with pants and shirts, everybody washing their own except Max, Lydia, and Ashlyn.

The days after the power went out Jean had observed, and almost enjoyed, the quiet. There was no buzz of a fridge cutting in, the washer and dryer remained mute and empty, the toaster didn't pop, and the microwave no longer binged. Sounds now consisted of crackling wood and mingled voices as they worked at the jobs required so that they all could get through. Water became an issue due to the well being artesian. They'd uncovered the old drinking well when the temperatures rose.

"Gotta be careful of wiggle-tails," Max had cautioned as he lifted the rotting lid off it.

"What are riggle tails, Poppy Max?" Ashlyn had asked, eyes large.

"Little worms in the water. I remember them from when I was a boy. Got to strain it and boil it. Make it safe for drinking."

Jean had scrunched up her nose, disgusted at the thought of worms. But what choice did they have? So, boiling water became a constant chore. They did it for laundry, bathing, drinking, and everything but flushing. They could only flush the toilet as needed and after the first while, until they knew the electric was gone for good, the taps had been left to run. Once they realized the power would not return any time soon, they drained every bit they could out of them. The pump needed power, so the pipes were emptied to prevent freezing. Five-gallon buckets lined along one wall, then boiled regularly which required the stove to be filled and stoked no matter how warm the kitchen got. Conservation was now a way of life.

Though they preserved every possible bit of food they could, it appeared they would run out sooner than expected. The large crowd made the potatoes, turnip, and carrots all but vanish, but beans and lentils were still in store at Jean's. They provided nutrition and were filling.

Some people were running far lower around town and Jean was losing the ability to help with her own supplies becoming sparse. She now only cooked vegetables twice a week. She made a large stew once a week and a big dinner on Sunday. There was no milk, butter, or fresh green vegetables. They lived on what they had and what they could hunt.

Laundry sorted, Jean and Mallory had cleaned the kitchen and were about to sit for a cup of weak tea. RJ and Max entered the house just as Ashlyn came out of the bedroom. "Mommy is dead," she said, her large eyes solemn.

Jean ran to the bedroom and the men followed while Mallory took little Ashlyn by the hand and led her to the table. "Are you sure?" she asked the child, her voice soft. Ashlyn nodded.

In the other room, Jean and RJ approached Lydia's bed and he reached out and touched her cold skin. Jean looked at him and he nodded. Max moved forward, straightened the woman's body and moved her hands to cross over her chest.

"How long, Max?"

"She's not stiff yet, so not long," Max replied. "We need to clean the body. RJ, can you and Jean get the box? I'll do that. I've seen it done." Max had watched his mother clean many bodies when he was a small boy in the mid-seventies. Up until later in that decade there had been no funeral parlour on the island and the locals took care of their own and his mother often stepped up. Eventually the dead were all shipped off to the funeral home on the mainland, but that was impossible these days, so Max's knowledge became very valuable.

"There is a dress there, hung up for her. And shoes. We should bury her right away. I will make up a death certificate. Call Roy Pearcey to do a short service. Lydia was Anglican. Not that that matters anymore." Jean walked to the closet and pulled out the items.

She drew in a deep breath. Now for the hard part. She walked out of the bedroom and towards the child whose eyes filled at the nod of confirmation that the only mother she'd ever known was gone. Tiny tears plopped, one after the other onto her cheeks.

"I know, darling, it's sad." Jean reached for her.

"She's dead like the seagulls. We are all going to die from the poison." Ashlyn ran into her arms and sobbed.

"How do you know about the seagulls?" Jean asked, stroking her hair.

"I saw them at the beach yesterday. They're all over the place down by the cove where the caplin comes in."

Mallory looked at Jean. "Is that true?"

"They were dead by the ferry. I didn't know they were dead here."

"Everything is dying, Aunt Jean. And we will too. I miss my mommy." Then she was three, frightened and sad. Her wisdom gave way to the tiny broken heart that beat in her thin chest. She wrapped herself tighter against Jean's body and sobbed. Jean's latent maternal instinct fluttered to the surface, and she rocked and soothed her, with a low *shshshsh* accompanied by her own tears. Lydia had been a wonderful woman, taking her grandchild to raise late in life and she'd dealt with the likely death of her only daughter in the St. John's explosion with a strength that remained steadfast even in her days of pain and the new decline of her health from this strange malady that more than half the town now suffered with.

RJ slipped out the door, to go get the coffin. In preparation for Lydia's death, the men had made a rough casket out of hand tools that were in the old museum. They'd been building a supply although Lydia's was the first death. All the old items were being rediscovered now that lack of electricity bore the new useless. Old men, Max's age, were advising until they were too sick to do so anymore.

We're leaving, Jean thought, after he'd gone. *He's right. We're going to have to go.*

She considered what Ashlyn had told her about the gulls. Was the wild food the reason that people were sick? Those with food in stock, like her household, were healthier. Yes, they'd had some seal and seabirds fresh, but they'd bottled most of it before things were too contaminated. Perhaps the canning process killed whatever made people sick. They couldn't explain Lydia's illness other than the fact that she had already been sick and so perhaps couldn't battle whatever little got in her system.

Now with Lydia gone, they could leave. Nothing impeded them as a sick person had. She hadn't had the opportunity to ask RJ why he wanted to go it alone instead of with all the other boats if they chose to go. But she would get the answer from him soon because if the gulls were dead in the cove, the salmon and lobster they counted on to get them through the spring and summer likely were too. Then there was the large American vessel anchored offshore, a floating reminder of their vulnerability.

She stroked Ashlyn's hair. Her sobs subsided to a gentle cry. Jean kissed the top of her little head. Yes. They'd take this child to safety, get her to Canada. And they would do it soon. Before they all died here like Lydia had and so many others were on track to do.

CHAPTER FOURTEEN

When Jean was a child in Toronto, she once attended the funeral of a friend's grandfather. The decorated war veteran died at 104 years old. The room that day was filled with family and friends, not one of them old enough to be a peer of the dead man. But he had lived a long and successful life and the gathering had become less sad, more celebratory as the day wore on. After the ceremony there was a gathering at which two portraits of the old soldier flanked either end of a table and in the centre a brass urn, polished to a gleam, contained all that remained of Omar Sara.

While the family milled around, Jean had been struck by the thought of a man, fighting the good fight against his old countrymen, surviving, and living such a long life after. It also occurred to her that while his life had seemed long, it nevertheless had been reduced to grey dust in a bronze jar. Nothing left of it but crumbs, nothing useful, nothing permanent.

Now, today, she was having similar feelings. Lydia, a woman widowed at a young age, her only daughter a drug addict, her granddaughter her last chance to fix things, had not lived the so-called successful life of Omar Sara, an old man who had risked life and limb to preserve democracy. Yet there she was, as well, reduced to nothing after all her years. She cleaned the room where Lydia had died and thought, such different lives, both reduced to dust.

The thinness of the line between *here* and *not here* was painfully obvious to Jean as she lifted the mattress and stripped the bedding. Lydia, who would be laid next to two more residents who also succumbed to the nuclear flu, was to be nothing but a memory to an insignificant few. Or maybe not. Who knew if any of them would survive to remember her?

Whether they stuck it out on Desolate Island and lived a small, quiet life until they died, or threw themselves at the mercy of the sea, brave like Omar, their end would be the same. Who knew which choice would give them more time?

Jean pondered it all as she removed the mattress cover as well, dreading the thought of scrubbing the vinyl-lined wrap. She had several pots of water on the stove. The women of the town had taken Ashlyn with them and the other adults were off on different missions leaving Jean alone in her house. She basked in the silence. The guests were considerate and pulled their weight but still, being alone was a treat.

Once the water heated, Jean scrubbed the sheets with a tiny bit of detergent until her hands were sore and her back ached. RJ returned in time to help her rinse them in the clear water and then they wrung them. The wind had dried the other clothes on the line by that time and they brought the clean sheets in, putting out the dead woman's bedding. It was ten degrees Celsius, and the breeze left the sheets fragrant and soft.

"I had no idea how much work it would be without the

appliances. Laundry is the worst," she grumbled, clearing up the water that had splashed around the floor.

RJ threw some tea bags on the table. "Traded for them with Layden Fancy for a bottle of turr!"

"Oh, put the kettle on, I'll sit with you in a minute." As he did so, Jean pulled out pans to grease. She had gotten cooking spray on sale at Costco at her last trip to St. John's and had bought a dozen cans. She used it sparingly, like they rationed the toilet paper that she also got at a discount and bought in bulk.

"The things you take for granted. I, for one, would love to shave." He set the kettle to boil then rubbed his chin, the beard there thick. He had always used an electric razor and so hadn't shaved in a long time.

"I like it," Jean smiled and ran a palm across his fuzzy cheek. They'd fallen into such a comfortable closeness over the past while, an unexpected blessing in these hard days.

"It itches, but it saves me time." He jutted his chin out.

"We're going?" Jean asked, heart leaping.

"Yeah, we have to go."

"You spoke to the ship?" He'd been trying to contact them.

"I called, no response. I can't find their frequency." Or they were ignoring him, he thought.

"When?"

"Soon. There are dead fish on top of the water. Half a dozen seals are on shore over in Back Cove, Max thinks they're sick too. I think we need to plan, pack up the supplies we have left, and leave. The weather is improving. There are no guarantees, but the engine is good. I've got Cleanfuel stored in the holds, every bit I could find, enough to take us there and back."

Soon. Jean rolled the word in her mind, then looked around at her house. How could she leave her sanctuary? But it made no sense to stay. Lydia was dead. There was poison in the air and the sea. But the ocean was an unknown as there were no weather forecasts. There were rumours of enemy ships in the area. It was hard to know what to do.

"There is serious talk about the other boats going too. Just loading up and taking everybody." Jean set about getting teacups.

"I heard. Let them go, I'd like them to go first to be honest," RJ said.

"Really? Why?"

"Because we need to be as small a target as possible."

"Target?"

"Yeah, we have to assume the water is full of warships, mines, who knows what else."

"So that's not a rumour?"

"That ship's not out there for no reason." RJ glanced at the window in the direction of the US navy boat.

"If they go first, that'll tell us where the threat is?"

"Or if there is any at all. It might be fine," RJ continued.

"Wait! So, all the people, our friends in this community, you want them to go off and get killed first so we know how to not get killed?" Shocked and appalled, she pulled out a chair and sat. Did he really want to literally test the waters with their friends?

"That's not fair, Jean. I would hope we would all survive the crossing, but I want to be a smaller target. If we all left together, we would be a bigger blip on a radar, might get mistaken for an attack. I think we would have better luck if we were one boat."

"Just everybody in this house and your father?"

"Colin's family too. Dad's grown attached to them and wouldn't leave without them. I know him by now. Plus, we need the nurse."

"The Maxes?" She was fond of the neighbours and couldn't dream of leaving them behind or sending them with other people.

"Yes, them too. I know it's a lot, but with the holds cleared out and bunks built in, we'll be fine."

"Half of the people will be dead soon. People won't leave behind sick family members."

"I know. Rick Palmer died today and the Slade boy. That's why I think we should go soon. We have nobody sick. We need to leave before we do."

"Oh, Jesus. Poor Maureen. That child was her whole world. He was only seven. When is soon?" Jean sipped the tea RJ set before her. Her stomach knotted at the news of two more deaths. One a child. She thought of little Ashlyn. Yes, three-year-old kids could die. Her heart cracked a little.

"Two days from now? If we can get packed up in time and weather allowing. We'll leave at night. Be well out in the gulf by the time the sun rises and far away from that warship.

"That fast? When do we tell the others? I assume you don't want to tell the entire town."

"No. Just our crowd. I'll invite everybody here for dinner. We'll tell them then. Give them some time to decide, pack some things."

"What if they don't want to go?"

"We'll leave them. But they'll want to go."

They heard steps outside. Max entered, the door staying open, the sheets on the line blowing dry in the island wind at his back.

"They're coming." His concerned eyes met RJ's, then Jean's.

"Who is coming?" Jean asked, standing and going to him. Max looked frail and ready to collapse. He glanced out the door towards the water, then back at them.

Jean knew then, exactly who he was referring to.

CHAPTER FIFTEEN

RJ handed the binoculars to Jean and turned to the crowd gathered in the kitchen. She'd relented and let Max use up some of the charge on her car to drive around and collect people. It seemed important.

"It's an amphibian ship so they launched smaller vessels and yes, they are coming this way. I think we'll see them in ten to twenty minutes. I don't know where they'll dock, but my guess is the government wharf. I think we need to greet them as a community. I think the mayor should take charge and we should all provide a united front. It doesn't look like an attack. These are Americans and last I heard we are still allies, even if we didn't join the war with them yet. Well, that we know of."

Reg cleared his throat. Mallory shuffled in her chair. The others stood around quietly listening.

"Let's not panic," Jean said. "These are the Americans coming, not the Russians or the Chinese or whoever our enemy is right now. We know so damned little, could be the British or the Norwegians at this point. We might be able to get some information out of them at least. I'm heading to the government wharf. Who's going with me?"

Mallory, not interested in being in a crowd that might include Francis, offered to stay with Ashlyn and Matt while the others scrambled to get dressed.

***

Loose pans of ice left over from the floes dotted the harbour that served as the hub for the boats. The wind whipped their faces. As predicted, the grey, flat vessel carrying half a dozen American Naval soldiers docked at the rundown government wharf shortly after they arrived to greet them. Two men stepped up and onto the platform, faces serious but not unfriendly.

Jean stepped forward and introduced herself, professional, if suspicious. She held out her hand. "Jean Adler, mayor of Desolate."

"I'm Lieutenant Wasburg. It's a pleasure to meet you and wonderful to know there are people out here. How are you making out?" He held her palm briefly. His hand was warm, and his soft southern dialect reminded her of the voices of old country singers. Not being a fan of that music, she wasn't reassured.

"We've had a rough time," Jean said. "To be honest, we've got a lot of people sick, a number of them have died. We can only assume there were atomic bombs dropped and we're dealing with radiation because we have no idea. Gander and St. John's? Nothing in Corner Brook?"

Not confirming or denying it was radiation killing them, he said, "Just the east coast for now, ma'am. It was the Russians. There isn't much left of the major centres and the outlying areas have had people dying in great numbers according to our reports, however, as you can imagine, we're not going to head over there to check, the contamination is too high. In fact, we're measuring the pollution levels here and it's not good. There seems to be a decrease over the past couple of weeks but not enough to prevent serious illness in most people."

"Is it in the food chain then?"

"Yes, I think it's safe to say things are contaminated. You're not sick yet, yourself?"

Jean shook her head to indicate she wasn't. Before she could carry on, a man's voice intruded on their conversation.

"Do you have supplies for us? Food?" Francis Richmond walked into their group and Jean saw that behind him a large contingent of citizens followed.

"Sir, no we don't. We only have enough supplies for our crew. However, we can radio a Canadian ship to see if they can bring humanitarian aid this way. Word is one is on the way from up north. The Canadian ships are mostly in the pacific."

"Figures," Francis spat. "That useless crowd in Ottawa protect their precious Vancouver before they can bother with us."

"I think they're spread pretty thin, Francis." Jean looked to Lieutenant Wasburg for confirmation.

"They are," the soldier confirmed. "I can't go into details of the military operations, but Canada has now officially joined the war, after this attack. Though they still are only aiding us with defense."

"Defense?" Jean inquired.

"Yes, patrolling these waters. There are warships just the northeast and eastern coast. Enemy submarines too. Russian mainly."

"So, all out war might happen here? In this province?" Jean asked.

"Ma'am, all due respect, there already is all-out war here. You have been seriously attacked."

"I mean, there's more to come?"

"Yes. Ma'am. I imagine so."

"Will it go around to the west coast of the province

too?"

"I wouldn't rule anything out. We're protecting your mainland now after this loss."

"The mainland? You mean Canada's mainland, right? Not the Island of Newfoundland. You're calling Newfoundland a loss? You've lost the province and now you're preventing further encroachment into Canada? Is that accurate, sir?" RJ asked.

"You understand, there isn't much left to...look sir, I know it sounds terrible and we only follow orders and don't know the larger strategy. We're doing our best."

"And the new president? She's capable?" Somebody'd gotten a brief five minutes of static-filled news on the radio the day Lydia died. Hardly anybody had heard of Briar McAdams, but somehow, she had become president of the United States. The country needed a stable voice and hers rung out as the most cohesive and best option to negotiate an end to the conflict.

"She is the Commander in Chief, and we follow her directions. Honestly though, sir, there is no winning this war. The destruction is beyond what you can imagine. The most we can hope for is to stop it and rebuild. I can't stay, sir, we'll have to get back to the ship. We thought we should check out the community and let you know we do have you covered. I'd avoid eating any of the local game though. Hopefully you can get some supplies soon to get you through."

"What's the gulf like, sir? And up around the northern peninsula? Ice? Warships?" RJ asked.

"Nothing we're aware of. We were told there would be ice in these waters well up until May, but the radar is showing it's all pretty much gone."

"The ice is usually heavier and earlier, but it's been

gone earlier these past few years, same as the water levels are still rising. Things have changed a lot." RJ said.

"Climate change, yeah." The officer nodded.

"Wasn't a hoax," RJ said, his expression wry.

"Never thought it was, sir," he replied. The American, Lieutenant Wasburg, looked out at the crowd. There were signs of exhaustion and illness among them. Several people coughed. He shook his head. Jean caught the haunted look in his eyes. This man had seen more than he was letting on.

"Can we speak privately?" Jean requested.

"What the hell—" Francis started but RJ silenced him with a warning look.

Wasburg glanced from Jean to Francis. "Yes, certainly, ma'am," he said.

"Thank you for coming ashore," Jean said when she had him far enough away from the grumbling gathering. "It's hard to be out here alone with no news. I didn't want to panic the town, but I have a question and perhaps you can advise me. Some of the people are talking of leaving in the fishing boats, going across to Nova Scotia or even Quebec and well, I'm undecided if that's the best way forward or if we should stick it out. What would be your advice?"

"Ma'am, I'm not sure it's my place to give advice but honestly, this place is poison." He looked around at the beautiful bay, absorbing the blue of the sky, the slap-slosh of water against the dock, rhythmic and soothing, completely at odds with his words. "I say leave the sick and go. Over time, I can't see anybody surviving if they stay. But, if you decide to go, go fast. There could be some heavy battles in these waters in the next few days and week."

"Okay, thank you," Jean responded. "Anything details? Any information is helpful. It gives us a chance to make the right decision. Anything you think might help, what harm can it do to tell us?"

He looked hard into her face. She just wanted to help her town survive. This raggedy gang looked like they wouldn't last another month in the place. He waffled. Then decided.

"I could be court martialed for saying this, but word is that something big will happen within a week. I cannot tell you what it is. I'd get to the other side of this gulf as fast as you can. The weather looks very good for the next few days but there is some movement, possible storm activity coming up in about four or five days as well. It's what? A, four or five-day trip in those boats? Do y'all have enough fuel to make it?"

"There is probably enough fuel left in this town to take three or four of the boats across. It would be crowded but leaving behind the sick—I know, that sounds so awful."

"It's awful but it's the truth. Don't take the sick and dying. Land in Quebec, it's closer, make sure you have ID, there have been border trouble from American refugees, then once you are there, head north where there are no military targets. If you were my family, that's what I'd tell you to do. Stay away from larger cities and military bases. Avoid Petawawa, Bagotville, Borden, places like that. Toronto and Montreal too. They're all potential targets should this escalate. Go to a rural area if you can."

"Thank you so much." Jean's heart pounded. What was coming? She dared not even consider the possibilities. "I appreciate this. It's important we know before we set out, what we're looking at."

"Good luck, Mayor."

"Thank you." She briefly wondered if she should salute or something but instead nodded. "You're welcome to come up for a cup of tea," she offered, hospitality as much a part of her as her arms and legs. She mentally counted the teabags. They had enough to make a good pot. Her stash of sugar and Carnation milk jammed under her bed would make an appearance if he accepted.

"Sounds nice, ma'am but we have to get back. Orders." He smiled then, and though older than Jean, there was something of a boy in him, one that had vanished with the start of a military career but appeared when a familiar home-made friendliness was directed his way.

They walked back to the dock. RJ's eyes questioned her. She gave a small shake of her head. Later. He could wait. Francis, not so much.

"What are you cooking up with the Americans? You got some sort of scheme going on?"

The lieutenant walked past and gave Jean a sympathetic look as he climbed back aboard the small tender where his crewmates waited. He turned and gave a friendly, informal salute and then sat while the crew pulled the craft away.

"Francis, bugger off. I asked about medical supplies, if there was medicine for the sick," she lied. "I didn't want to discuss peoples' personal medical conditions in public. Plus, I didn't want to put him on the spot in front of everyone if he had to give bad news or say no."

"What did he say?" Reg asked, coming over to her, a skinny cigarette dangling from his lips, self-rolled from the last of the tobacco in town.

"He said they don't have any medical supplies. He's contacting the Canadian ship." More lies but until she talked to RJ alone, she wasn't comfortable talking about the officer's recommendation. Half her community had a terminal illness and would need to be left behind. She knew many would not leave them.

Max went home by himself, to fill Mallory in. Jean expected another run in with Francis but other than sidelong looks he left her alone. He hadn't shown up to harass Mallory which was starting to get worrisome. There was no way he would just let her leave without some reaction.

After getting updates from people around town, including the news of several more deaths, Jean and RJ walked through the remaining crowd who fell in behind them, forming a forlorn parade, eyes sunk deep in haunted faces, feet scuffing along the pavement. They separated off into their laneways and houses with a wave until it was just her and RJ walking to her place alone.

As soon as they were out of sight, he reached down and took her hand. His palm was warm in the cool spring air. She turned to him, and he looked down at her, searching her face.

"Tell me, "he said.

And so, she did.

CHAPTER SIXTEEN

At life's beginning, things are counted in firsts. The first tooth, first step, first word, first day of school, and so on. At its concluding days, it's counted in lasts. There is a final Christmas, one more birthday, the last breath.

This was the first time Jean had strolled with a man, holding hands, feeling a love that had evaded her for most of her adult life. A decade of studies, a demanding career in the corporate world, and no time for a personal life had left her out of luck. By the time she had reached her mid-thirties, she'd given up on love.

Now a good man had fallen into her life. She loved him. Oh, she loved all her guests, but she particularly cared for this man who warmed her bed at night and kept her from going insane in this new and foreign reality.

The sun was high and warm, the blue sky its normal colour. She averted her head, so she couldn't see the scar on the horizon that was a naval vessel and a smaller dark speck moving towards it carrying the soldiers back. She remained quiet. Savouring. Pretending. Denying. She wanted to enjoy this first. But she couldn't. When her great grandmother died many years ago, the minister read a verse from Revelations in The Bible at her funeral. It popped into Jean's mind as she walked along.

And he said unto me, it is done. I am Alpha and Omega, the beginning, and the end. I will give unto him that has thirst of the fountain of the water of life freely.

Their water was polluted, even that of the ever-vast ocean that had supplied a livelihood to this place for centuries. There was no life in it anymore, its bright blue depths sullied. How she had adored the humpbacks that had played off her cove as she watched them from the deck. How enamoured she'd been of the schools of porpoises that sometimes traveled past, their curving dives forward, synchronized to perfection, a delight to her come-from-away heart.

Now they needed to swim west, or north, or wherever the water was clean. If there remained such a place.

The Bible verse spoke of heaven, not earth. But this place was her paradise, an escape from the hell of depression that had nearly stolen her life and ended her career. It had helped her throw out the medication once her mind healed, freed from the stress imposed upon it.

She could sure use a damned Prozac now, however.

"Teabag for your thoughts?" RJ's voice interrupted her musing.

"What?" she laughed. "A teabag?"

"Well pennies have no value, and a good Tetley is worth a fortune these days."

The laughter helped prepare her to answer the question she'd been able to avoid for a few moments.

"We have to go. And soon. The American guy said we should go before more Russian warships arrive and they're coming in days, perhaps no more than a week's time. He wouldn't say precisely what is happening or when, but that's what I read into his words."

"I thought that's what you were discussing."

"It's my opinion that we should all go together as a convoy. I think it'll be safer."

"I still think you're wrong on that." RJ's voice was firm.

"Why? Why do you want us to go alone? Why don't you want to stay with the community? Take the risk. You might be wrong you know."

"I don't know, it's what I want to do. Let's call it intuition." He took a different tact. "Look, it makes sense. You're the mayor, you should see them off first, make sure those left behind have as much as we can give them, then we go ourselves."

"Or should I be on the lead boat, taking them across?"

RJ stopped. He drew in a breath, exasperated. "Okay, I'll say it straight out. My mother, God love her, used to say that the biggest truths have the smallest words. Well, here it is. I want to live. I want you and my father to live. I want Ashlyn to most of all because she might be the only shot of anyone from Desolate Island talking of its existence in the future. I confess I want that more than I want us to survive. But to have that, I think we'll have to go alone. Look, I want the people I love the most around for a long time. Does that make me a bad person? Probably. But that's it. I think our chances are better out there alone. I just do."

The roar of the sea filled the quiet while Jean absorbed his words.

"No, you're not a bad person. Okay, let's prepare to leave, after the others are gone." She understood his reasons and trusted in his instincts. Her battle was with right and wrong. But did right and wrong even exist anymore?

"I probably am a bad person, Jean. But I'm comfortable being that. If it gets us out of here alive. My hope is we all make it out. And we likely will. If they're going to make it, they'll make it without us, right?"

"You do make sense. And no, I don't think you're a bad person. I mean, before all this I thought you were a bit of a troublemaker, a good-for-nothing who wasted his gifts here in this town. But you've stepped up like nobody else has, you've been walking this town, checking on people, helping, bringing information. I couldn't have made it this far without you. Well, at least not without losing my mind."

"You're sharing your bed with me. You will never ever convince me you've not lost your mind."

"You may have a point," she said, chewing her lip, serious.

"Hey!" He laughed and pulled her in for a kiss. "Maybe I should explain why I came back here, back home, in the first place."

"Yeah, why did you?"

"Well, you see, while I did get well-educated, and as much as I loved to learn and later, once I started working, earning money, I started to get depressed. Turns out none of it made me happy. I think I had an early mid-life crisis, because I burned out hard and fast. I always say I came home to spend time with Dad after his heart attack and didn't want to leave him. But that's only partly true. The fact is I discovered that I love it here. I still don't want to leave. I know how much money I could have made if I had stayed working instead of coming home and helping my father fish. Jeez, I think *he* reminds me every day. And I admit I drank too much, drove too fast and acted juvenile for a man in his thirties, but I didn't get to do that in my teens because I was so driven to succeed in school and work, to get the hell out of here as soon as I finished Grade Twelve. Now though, this situation. Well, I grew up fast. And as much as I want to stay, the peace has been stolen from Desolate Island, Jean. War is a thief and it's just not home anymore in the same way."

"We're a lot alike. That's why I came here. I too burned out on a career. It's why I love it so much."

"What good would a job in St. John's do me now anyway? I'd be dust in the atmosphere, glowing orange in the night sky."

"Turns out you made the best choice by following your heart, yeah." Jean had been older, with a good solid balance in her bank account before becoming a hermit here. But she understood his need to escape.

"Do you think money will still be good in Canada?" she asked.

"I don't know, I would imagine so. Not that I have any. I'll find work. I'm overqualified for a ton of jobs."

"Well, I have oodles," Jean informed him. Her frugality had kept her living off the interest of her savings for years.

"What? I heard you spent every cent on the house and live off the land out of necessity? Word is you're so tight with money that you squeak like a dog toy. The island grapevine must have a transmission line down!"

"Well, that's kind of what I told people. I live very frugally. I don't need much. Plus, it discouraged advances from the gold diggers."

"Yeah, that makes sense. I can think of a number of men who would go after a beautiful woman, because she's got money." He felt a twinge of guilt. He'd first aligned with her because she had the most supplies. Funny how currency changed once they were without a means to spend money. Now he was happy she'd allowed him into her life, whatever was left of it.

"Jean, I love you." He kissed her on the lips, so she wouldn't have to say it back. He didn't want her to feel that pressure. He just needed her to know.

"RJ."

"No, listen, the world is most likely ending, we don't know what tomorrow is going to send us, but I have feelings for you that can only be described as love. You're the strongest woman I've ever known, and you keep me sane. Lately, with all the people sick and dying, I've nearly lost it. My God, it's so hard to live like this. I want to go to bed some days and not ever get up. But you, you just do everything that needs to get done. You feel how hard it is too, I've heard you cry in your room, but you pick yourself up and just get back to it. And you are so good with Ashlyn, so kind. You save me every time when I want to throw it all down. When I want to give up, you say or do something, fix something, laugh at something, that keeps me moving forward. Sorry. I know, it's all so soon, I'm intense. I should stop being so intense, right? Forget it, let's just go home."

"Don't be foolish, RJ. Yes, you're intense but this is a crazy situation. Funny thing though." She hesitated a moment. "I was thinking the same about you." She smiled up at him. Relishing this moment of happiness.

He kissed her again, deep, and hard. Relieved. Happy. "Bit late for romance, isn't it?"

"Bit late for everything, but that doesn't mean we shouldn't have it in the time we have. And who knows, perhaps we'll live long lives in upper Canada." She winked at him.

"I hope so, Jean, I'd like to live a long life with you. In for a penny...so here goes. Want to get married when we get there? Maybe adopt Ashlyn? Time is not for the wasting, Jean. I want to marry you." His serious eyes devoured hers. Begging her for a yes.

"It would be a bit foolish to ask for some time to think about it, so yes, let's do that. I think we could make a marriage work and I think Ashlyn deserves any normal life we can make for her, if we make it there." She would grab this happiness by two hands, live her last days on earth as something she never expected to be. A fiancée.

And if luck allowed a wife.

"Thank you," RJ said. They weren't the right words, but gratitude was the premier emotion of the moment. RJ kissed her again, his hand coming up around her jawbone, her thin face lifted to his, breathing into him, accepting him and his offer.

"Let's go, we have a lot to do."

Was this Alpha or Omega, she wondered as they walked together, holding hands, up the stretch of quiet road to her house in the harbour. Perhaps it was both. She didn't care. Either way, they were going to live the rest of their lives together, however long or short they might be.

CHAPTER SEVENTEEN

A short while after RJ and Jean arrived home, the house was filled with all inhabitants accounted for. Ashlyn's eyes were large and sad these days which had the adults constantly seeking ways to cheer her up, keep her busy, and console her.

"Feels like spring, don't it?" As self-declared dish cleaner, Max wiped up some crumbs from the table and busied himself at the sink, washing every plate and bowl with a precision born of a pure desire to be helpful.

"It was nice to wake up to chirping this morning." Spring birds had returned from the south and seemed to thrive in the contaminated air — for now, but RJ didn't hold out much hope for their survival long term.

"Tom Cat caught one, but I took it from him. I don't want him to eat anything like that." The cat rubbed around Jean's ankles at his name.

"Will Tom and Princess go on the boat too?" Ashlyn asked, leaning down and stroking Tom's fur.

"Oh, yes, can't leave Tom Cat behind. He's family," Jean said.

"And so is Princess. She's my sister," Ashlyn said. "I wanted a real baby sister, but Mommy said a fur-sister would have to do at her stage in life."

The adults suppressed a smile. She would get mad if they laughed at her, amused by her adult vocabulary. When she was able to control her laughter, Jean responded, "Women can only have babies up to a certain age, it's true, and fur babies certainly are fun. That's why I have Tom. Of course, I got lucky because now I have you to take care of too."

"But I'm not a baby," she insisted, petting Tom from head to the tip of his tail so that his butt lifted when she smoothed over it.

"No, you're a delightful young lady," RJ said.

Max wrung out the dishcloth and hung it on a hook. He left the water in the sink, hot could be added to it later if something needed to be cleaned. He was ever diligent to conserve whatever of that precious commodity was brought into the house, the toting of buckets being such hard work.

"Game of five-hundreds?" Jean asked, grabbing the deck of cards off the top of the refrigerator. Before anyone could answer, RJ jumped up.

"Do you hear that?"

"What?"

"Shhhh!"

The house grew quiet and a moment later Jean picked up the sound. She met RJ's eye.

"Stay here," she advised. "Somebody is out at the cellar. RJ and I will go."

"I'll watch out the back window. They won't see me," Max said.

"Keep quiet, stay busy."

"Is it 'mericans?" Ashlyn whispered.

"I don't think so, sweetheart, we've been watching for them and they wouldn't get here that fast. Probably teenagers."

"Come to me," Mallory offered, arms open.

RJ went through the back door, handing Jean her jacket, throwing on his own and grabbing his rifle along the way. He shoved a box of ammunition in his pocket.

"You think we need the guns?" Jean whispered, with a glance back towards the main part of the house.

"Better safe than sorry."

"Jeez, yeah, guess so," Jean said. She grabbed a loaded rifle off the rack. Just in case, they'd all been loaded as a precaution after making sure the rack was too high for Ashlyn to reach.

Jacket on, she tucked the gun under her arm, feeling ridiculous and terrified all at once. They were in a war, but everybody here was her neighbour, her friend. Weren't they?

They made their way towards the root cellar, the night dark but the perpetrators visible as shadows. Jean and RJ knelt behind a small bush, put the rifles to their shoulders and waited.

"What the f—," Francis Richmond hollered when the first explosion occurred. He ran out from the cellar, terror in his voice as he made for the road.

"Your booby traps worked!" Jean whispered.

"Shh, there's the truck. Can you see who it is?"

"It's Francis' truck, but somebody else is driving it. It's coming this way. Must be nice to have fuel to waste."

Layden Fancey jumped out and they could hear a whispered argument between the two men. Layden appeared to want to leave, but Francis wasn't convinced.

"Damn, I thought I could trust Layden," RJ whispered.

"What do we do? He's got a rifle too."

The men came closer, Layden with a gun under his arm and Francis coming behind him. They crouched down further to avoid detection. The two men had to have known that they would have company after the trap tripped, so it appeared they were ready for a showdown. They kept glancing at the house though, not realizing Jean and RJ were already on the other side of the cellar.

RJ stood, aimed the rifle, and pressed a finger against the trigger.

"I don't want to kill you, but guess what? I will," he stated, his voice cold and strong.

Both men pivoted in their direction. Jean remained crouched.

Layden held his gun under his arm, raised it ever so slightly, and RJ issued a warning. "Move again and I'll shoot. Now what are you doing? What do you want?"

"Jeez, RJ, b'y. We needs some grub. We're starving." Laydon's voice was pleading.

"So instead of asking, you decide to rob us in the dead of night?" RJ asked.

"I've come for my wife too," Francis declared.

"You didn't tell me that," Layden said. "We were supposed to get a few spuds and stuff for the trip."

"She doesn't want anything to do with you," RJ said, ignoring Layden.

"That's a lie. I want to hear from her myself."

"It's not a lie," a voice shouted from the house. "I don't want to see you and if you come around here again, I'll shoot you myself."

"You, useless piece of sh—I'll come in the middle of the night and strangle you while you sleep!" Francis said, turning to go towards the house.

Jean knew RJ couldn't take his gun off Layden, but

before she could stand up to do anything to stop his approach a shot rang out. It whizzed past Francis and struck his truck, *smash*, in the headlight.

"Trust me, I missed you on purpose," Max said, his voice coming from the direction of the house as well.

"I'd personally get in that one-eyed truck before he takes out another light, or worse," RJ advised the two men.

"Too slow, Francis," Max shouted from the window. Another ping and a crash as the second light blew it to smithereens.

"Get out, Francis. We have a closet full of ammunition," RJ lied.

"It's true." Jean stood, hoisted her gun at the men and aimed.

"You whore!" Francis shouted and this time it was Jean whose gun blasted into the night. It smashed a window.

"Sorry, what did you call me, Francis?" she asked.

"I think he said hoarder, you're a hoarder," RJ said. "At least that's what he'd better have said. Is that what you said, Francis?"

"Answer," Max demanded, "or I'll fire at your leg. You know I'm the best shot on the island." He wasn't lying. He had the reputation for being able to knock a turr on the wing, out of the sky like nobody else.

"Yes, that's what I said," Francis stammered. With three guns pointed at him, his bluster left, his anger needing to be swallowed. "We're leaving."

"You are, Francis. Layden is staying," RJ said.

"What?" Layden said. His voice quaked.

"That arse is going, but you're staying, Layden. Put the gun down, then head towards the house. Now."

The truck revved up and Jean rolled her eyes. The

thing guzzled Cleanfuel like a drunk at a cash bar and they needed every drop to fire up the longliners. The fact that Francis still had some in his truck meant that while all the town was pooling their supply to fill the boats' tanks, he was still holding on to his, so he could haul his lazy arse up the road to steal their food or to steal back his wife.

Layden placed the gun down as the truck sped off. He turned, head lowered, and Jean followed him, weapon aimed downward while RJ went back to the cellar to check on things. He stopped by to explain the racket to the neighbours before he headed to the house.

***

"I'm sorry, Jean," Layden said. He sat at the kitchen table with his head bowed.

"You have nothing left?"

"Not much. I thought... I don't know. I figured I could sneak a few items. Francis got me riled up, said you fellers had a cellar full and was holding back from everybody. The whole town is talking about that."

"Layden, we're pretty low ourselves. We have some food yes, but we also have a big crowd. We've been feeding the family next door and at Ralph's house too," Jean said.

"My boy isn't doing well. I thought perhaps a nice feed would help."

"Layden, I think you're right. Here." RJ came in with a bucket and laid it on the table. It was filled with potatoes. He pulled several jars of meat out of his pocket and put it beside the pail. "I'll put them in a bag for you, Layden. You go home, make some grub for that boy of yours. If you need more, come back. We don't have enough to feed everybody, but we would have done our best for you."

"I killed Maggie's chicken."

"What?"

"Last Sunday, I snuck in and stole the biggest one, chopped his head off, plucked him like a turr, and cooked him up. Savoury stuffing and all. No potatoes though, but it was still good."

"I heard one was missing."

"Yeah, I needed to feed the boy, and t'was her rooster, no eggs out of him for grub."

"Maggie's got to eat those chickens."

"Wants to take them on the longliner to Nova Scotia, she does."

"Jeez, somebody tell the woman we're in a war and starving."

"Well, her coop is pretty much a bunker, so they're not contaminated and I have to say, old Cocky tasted some good."

"Crispy?" RJ winked.

"Like bacon," Layden smiled, a wry gesture that wrenched at Jean's heart.

"We got lots of bread baked," Mallory said, hauling out a couple loaves and putting it on the table.

"I got a can of Carnation milk, and can spare a few teabags," Jean added.

"You got a can of Carnation? Sneaky bugger," RJ said, laughing.

"I was saving it for a special occasion. Nearly killing each other counts."

"Boys, I don't know what to say. I fooled up bigtime. I should have known Francis was blowing it out his arse. I'm sorry, Mallory, but you could have done a lot better than that arsehole."

"Oh yes, I know that now." Mallory had tears in her

eyes. It was good to be validated.

"Now get out, Layden, before we shoot you. Go home, feed your family," Jean ordered.

Soon, Layden was off with two bags of supplies, his shoulders slumped, the guilt of his attempted robbery not reduced by the kindness of his friends. He'd screwed up, resorted to theft rather than admit he was failing to feed his family and that was a mistake he'd have to live with for a long time.

If he lived a long time.

CHAPTER EIGHTEEN

Two days later, RJ came bounding into the house, grabbed Jean and planked a long kiss on her lips. His father was with him, a box of supplies in his hands. They were all in full swing, readying the boat for the trip.

"Layden's boy is better. He only had the flu!"

Ashlyn giggled from the table where she was eating boiled turnip and potatoes with bottled rabbit. She never complained about the food, only once longing for pizza but the cheese had been long consumed. Mallory turned and smiled, proud of the twelve loaves of bread that lined the countertop. The community was abuzz with plans to "bug out" as RJ called it.

"What? That's good news then!" Jean laughed. "What's got into you?"

"What, what? Can't I kiss my fiancée?"

"What is this now?" Mallory asked, a curious expression on her face.

Just at that moment, Max exited his bedroom, book in hand. Jean noted it was the Bible.

"Fiancée? Yoom getting married?" Max boomed, his voice happier than it had been in a while.

"Oh yes, weem getting married, minute we gets to Quebec and can work it out. We decided a few days ago but have been too busy to tell you," RJ said, his dialect matching Max's.

"RJ!" Jean scolded.

"Yoom ashamed of me, missus?" he joked, winking at Max.

"No, I just thought we'd tell people when we got to Quebec is all."

"Quebec? Sure, I can marry you two right here. I'm a Justice of the Peace remember?" Max said.

"What?" Jean turned to him.

"Sure, so is you, Jean. You can marry people. But I was the mayor one time and kept my certification up. I can marry folks, notarize stuff. I can marry the two of you here, or at sea. I'm a sea captain too, you know?" He grinned. He had never married anybody in all his life but always wished he could. The ministers had all the fun.

"Yes, I know I can, but I knew I couldn't marry myself to somebody. You really can?"

"If you can, then we're going to. Before we leave. I brought this." RJ pulled a small square cardboard box out of his pocket. The reason his shy father had come along was to witness, having handed over the box with a hesitant smile. "Mom didn't have much to leave so she left me her rings. I hope they fit. Mom was very small."

The ring was a bit big on Jean's left finger, only because she had lost so much weight. It was a tiny diamond, surrounded by smaller diamonds in a traditional setting. The matching band spooned into it in the box, but he gave her just the one.

"I got a wedding ring for you, RJ," Mallory spoke from beside the stove. She slipped off to the parlour and came back a moment later with a white gold band, diamonds circling the front of it. It was broad, a man's ring, and likely worth a tiny fortune.

"This isn't Francis', is it?"

"No, Dad's. From his second marriage. It lasted just a few months and he gave it to me to keep so the girl he married couldn't find it." Mallory had married Francis to escape the constant stream of women who came into her father's life. She had only been seventeen, eager to escape. Francis had a nice car and came from a well-to-do family like hers. Eventually he lost it all, and the anger of his downward spiral was taken out on her. She had never been able to count on her late father for support in any sense but financial, but there he took care of her well. The ring was part of a stash of items Francis had never seen. She was shocked he hadn't shown up again since the cellar, but RJ was a formidable force to face.

"So, wanna get 'itched?" RJ asked.

"Seriously? Now?"

"Now," Mallory said, "Let's get you ready, do it right. You need to change into a dress, put on some makeup. We need to have a nice dinner and celebrate. It's stew night."

"Come on, Mallory, we don't have time for all of that. We're getting ready to leave. We have to organize—"

"We do, but I was going to cook anyway, so we will. I'll be damned if we'll let this war steal all the happiness from us. We can take some time back. Let's take two hours, then have supper like we planned. It'll be the last wedding on Desolate Island. Should I ask the neighbours?"

The last wedding.

Omega.

"RJ?" Jean looked to him for guidance. He knew how close they were to preparations for the trip.

"Yes, let's take a couple of hours and do this. We have time to get ready after."

"Awesome! Ashlyn, you can be flower girl. We'll get a pretty dress. Come on ladies, let's go find stuff." Mallory seemed a different person having stood up to Francis. Empowered and free and determined to find happiness in any circumstance she could. But it was the look of pure joy on Ashlyn's face that sealed it for Jean. She had worked so hard to make her happy since her mother died, and if this ceremony, one she was going to do anyway, would keep those dimples in her cheeks, she'd marry friggin' Max.

"This is crazy," Jean said, but she went along, laughing as Max ushered RJ and Ralph out the door.

Lydia's clothes were still hanging in her closet and since she generally wore dresses or skirts, a pale-yellow frock was located there. Lydia was several inches taller than Jean which made the dress appear more formal than it was. Jean's fabric bin revealed ribbons and lace. A makeshift veil was fashioned and placed upon Jean's hair that was brushed and left long instead of in its usual fluffy ponytail. Mallory applied a bit of makeup on Jean, then herself. It had been a long time since she had worn any and she'd missed it.

"May I have some? Will there be cake?" Ashlyn asked.

Jean was about to say no as an old judgment of little girls and makeup popped into her mind. She had always been opposed to it, her feminist leanings seeing it as the road to the acceptance of objectification. How was that relevant anymore? Not much was when survival was the goal. The child might not live long enough to be old enough to wear makeup as an adult. Why not let her have her fun?

"You bet, Mallory will do you up like a grown-up woman," she responded and the light in Ashlyn's eyes was worth it. "There's no wedding cake, but we'll have the stew and bread."

"Mallory's bread is so good as cake, right, Aunt Jean?"

"You bet it is."

"You guys are making me blush," Mallory said, pleased.

RJ was back a short time later wearing his father's suit that hung a bit on the shoulders. Max wore a tie and carried an Anglican Church of Canada prayer book. He'd created a handwritten marriage registration for them both to sign.

"Let's make this quick, Max," Jean said, feeling a bit silly in the getup. She was not a dress person and never had dreams of a wedding like some girls. But Ashlyn's eyes were alight with joy and Mallory patted hers, moist with emotion, so she went along. The ceremony was fast, with RJ's eyes fastened to hers until they were pronounced husband and wife. Mallory used the A-Tab to capture photos and video. Though it had no signal, it had been shut down fully charged so that it sprang to life and recorded their ceremony in its tiny database. At least it still worked fine as a camera. They kissed, rings on their fingers, a strange happiness in their hearts.

The witnesses cheered.

"Are we sure this is legal?" Jean asked, taking the handmade certificate, and adding it to a buoyant waterproof camera pouch along with the A-Tab and the other devices. It held all their papers. Birth certificate, travel passports, vaccine passports, drivers licenses too. It would serve as proof of their Canadian citizenship when they arrived in port or, conversely, let people know who had been lost at sea if they didn't make it.

"Oh yes. We'll register it at Quebec. If they have any trouble, we'll do it again, but we shouldn't."

"Good enough for me," RJ said. "Let's go do the honeymoon." He pulled her arm towards the bedroom, and everybody laughed.

"I think we'll have supper, then load some more stuff into the boat," Jean said, her eyes happy, her mind practical.

"And already with the nagging," he joked.

"Hey, that's sexist," Jean scowled.

"It is, and we both know I'm the nagger in this marriage. But I wanted to try it on, get husbandly."

"Well, I'd get husbandly by being smarter than that." Jean winked and slapped his rear end.

"Already smarter, picked you for a wife."

"Ewww, corny," Marilyn from Max's house said as the family groaned, then laughed again. Jean went to help Mallory with supper. Max set the table and Ashlyn went to play with the cats. The Maxes and Ralphs were thrilled to be invited, eager as they were for normalcy. Since they were all going to leave the island soon, this was a farewell party as much as it was a wedding. Marilyn spotted the guitar on a stand in the living room.

"Yeah, it's mine. RJ plays it sometimes. I was teaching myself to play but lost interest." Jean answered Marilyn's inquiry about it. She needed a hobby in the long winters here and it seemed a fun way to pass the time.

Marilyn tuned the instrument, and her husband came to stand with her. "You have to have your first dance now."

RJ and Jean were nudged to the centre of the kitchen. With the table pulled back, the tiny space was just big enough for two people to move in each other's arms.

They broke into an old song, a slow melody. It might have been by Shania Twain. Jean didn't know old country music well. RJ made a big bow and Jean slipped into his embrace. She held tight and swayed with him. She willed herself to enjoy the moment, to not think about what this really was.

Another first. That might also be a last.

CHAPTER NINETEEN

A knock on the door from Reg ended the celebration. He stopped by to inform those gathered that they had decided to leave the following morning at dawn. Five boats would carry every single person who wanted to go. They would be crammed into the vessels, packed like sardines in the confined spaces of the smallest boats so that they burned the least amount of fuel. One would head up around the Northern peninsula, then down to Corner Brook, splitting off after they steamed so far south. The remainder would follow the same route but head across the gulf once they cleared the straits.

A pall fell over the crowd, the guitar set aside.

"You're still staying?" Reg asked.

"We are. At least for a while," RJ said with a glance at Max.

"We would like to have you with us, but we understand. We've assigned people to boats and we're loaded up pretty good. We'll go first thing after the sun rises. The water is as calm as I've ever seen in late May and now that the town has decided to go, they don't want to wait."

"How many staying?"

"Well over a hundred. They won't leave their sick and we can't crowd the boat with them. People are pissed off about that, but what can you do? You can't make the well stay behind or go with us so the dying can die someplace else."

"You're leaving your father, Reg?"

"He insists I go. He has wood and food and water. We set him up well. He's not going to last too long." Reg's voice grew grim with his choice.

"I'd do the same thing if Father was sick, Reg," RJ said, wondering if he would.

"I'd make you," Ralph Sr. said, his quiet voice firm.

"It's hard." Reg's eyes misted over. "But I got the youngsters to think of. I got to get them away from the poison. They're so thin now and probably already got some radiation. We were eating lots of rabbit and turrs before we knew, then we had next to nothing."

"I'm sure they're fine. But you're right to get them far away from here."

Jean walked over to her long-time friend. He'd tied her stage on in an act of generosity that she would never forget, saving her property. She wrapped her arms around him, her lemon-coloured dress swinging around her legs, her eyes wet from the thought of this dear man and the choice he'd been forced to make. Uncomfortable with displays of affection, he nonetheless wrapped his arms awkwardly around her back. He sobbed once into her shoulder, then stood, wiped his eyes, and grinned, trying to cover.

"Turning into a baby, I s'pose. Well anyway, we'll see you in Quebec. We'll be parley-vousing before you know it," he said.

Jean laughed, a welcome sound in a room ready to split abroad with emotion. "Yes, we will. Smooth sailing, my friend."

Reg shook hands with RJ, hugged the others, and

left. Jean didn't know if anyone else would come. There seemed to be a reluctance to say goodbye, to talk of the leaving at all, and many spoke of it as a temporary thing, until the war was over.

RJ had told the community they were staying behind for a bit to care for the crowd who did not wish to go. They knew that it would be thought of as selfish to cross alone immediately after the first boats left. The others in the house were aware of the plan and agreed to it but felt guilty at their lies. Jean also knew that some who stayed behind to care for an ailing child, parent or spouse thought that once their loved-one died they could go with RJ and Jean. They had no idea that they would leave in the middle of the night without letting anybody know. That final hope would be dashed with their departure.

Guilt swept over Jean, and she wrung her hands and moved to sit, heart heavy. She was their mayor, their leader, and she was taking the most comfortable way across to Quebec. She knew RJ was correct that it was best that they be the smallest target possible. But still, these were her friends and neighbours, people who had welcomed her to safety. She consoled herself that the crowded boats had a good chance of arriving safely on the Quebec shore. Ashlyn climbed into her lap and leaned against her.

The others turned away, their minds heavy too. They did not know the exact time RJ would leave and there had been a rustle of distrust at the secrecy, but RJ settled their concerns by simply saying that he just wanted to have enough time to pack.

"Some more of the lights are on out on the navy ship. It looks like it's closer too." He couldn't tell for sure, and it was too dark for binoculars to see much but the lights.

Jean carried Ashlyn into her room, placing her gently

in the bed where her grandmother had passed away not so long ago. Ashlyn didn't mind sleeping there, perhaps too young to grasp that most would be aghast at sleeping so soon in a bed where somebody died.

RJ watched her carry the child. He felt older now, grown up. Married. A father.

Jean came back, grabbed the binoculars from him and peered through, the adjustment taking a few seconds. Too dark to make out much but dim lights.

"Something has changed. Should you tell Reg and everybody else?" She lowered the spyglasses and her voice. The others had made their way to their beds, the dark a cue to their bodies that it was time to sleep.

"I don't want to bother them." RJ put them down, pulled Jean close. He put his face against her long hair, feeling the strands, soft against his cheek.

"I can't believe I have a family now," he whispered.

"Me either."

"Helluva thing to do in the middle of a war."

"Might be the only time it makes sense," she joked.

"I think you might be right. It's the only time in my life it's ever made sense and it's the only thing in my life that makes sense at all these days."

"It's good to have a friend in life." She snuggled tighter.

"It is indeed, m'love. And it's good for a child to have parents. I love that little girl like she's always been mine. Don't you?"

"Crazy, isn't it? I didn't think I had a maternal bone in my body."

"I love you, Jean. I'm glad we're together for whatever life we have."

"I love you too. And ditto. Bed?"

"Yeah, bed. It's our honeymoon and tomorrow morning I want to see Reg and the others off."

She took his hand and led him to their room.

Out the window the navy boat moved closer still, lights ablaze. Then about twenty minutes later its lights went out leaving nothing but millions of stars and a bright moon illuminating the small island community, the only sound that of the ocean lapping languidly against its rocky shores.

CHAPTER TWENTY

Roy Pearcey had quit school in grade eight. His story in later years, that he needed to do so to help his family, was utterly false. While he could manage to read, when words were required to come from his pen onto the paper, the letters jumbled, the sentences so senseless that there was no way he ever would be able to earn any of the many diplomas he dreamed of acquiring.

His oratory skills were discovered quite by accident. He attended a public meeting on the state of the fishery as a very young man and found himself frustrated by the tangential ranting of non-sequiturs at the politician sent to assuage the community. Roy, both angered and inspired, jumped up and described the crux of the issue in such clear and concise terms, and with such authority that he garnered a standing ovation from the gathering.

It lit a fire in him, the adulation like a drug, and so, to fulfil his desire to be heard, but unable to acquire the education required to do so, he became the lay reader of the Anglican Church. He filled in every other week when the current good reverend was in Addison's Bay, preaching at the other church that shared his oversight.

In recent decades the church attendance at Desolate Island had trickled to a handful-and-a-half, as the long-suffering minister, Reverend Adams, put it. Roy took joy out of the fact that the weeks he held service were as full as the weeks the actual minister preached. But on those Sundays, he noted the empty seats, the half-assed responses of the attendees to the order of service and mourned the days when filled pews had enthusiastically responded to his words.

The old Anglican church creaked in the wind, a fresh coat of paint and new shingles unable to hide the age of the stately building. It was mostly older people who attended the services out of habit and from lack of better things to do. But in the weeks since the attacks, there had been an uptick in attendance. The old church was opened regularly for services by the lay reader who felt that it was important to keep true to the faith they nearly all shared.

The bell peeled every Sabbath. Roy yanked the rope himself with enthusiasm so that an even toll at three in the afternoon each Sunday drew the parishioners back. It was an odd time for service, but one that allowed the church to warm up somewhat, and if the sun shone through the large windows, it suffused the altar in a golden light that somehow made up for the depressing lack of heat.

Today the church doors were closed, the bell unrung. Even Roy knew to curb his enthusiasm on a day like today. The service was being held on the government wharf. Jean and RJ held Ashlyn's hand, their faces cold in the early morning. The longliners' engines roared with power, a foreign sound in a place that had been quiet for so long now.

He had called together a blessing of the fleet. Each spring it was traditional to have this service, but he had never been the one to host, the minister having that honour. Now he stood, white robe flapping, sash pinned tight to keep it from winding around his body, his serious face hiding his glee at a chance such as this.

This was the ultimate blessing of the fleet. It was not sending the fishermen off with good luck. No, it was much more dramatic and important. It was sending his entire community off to sea. He knew there would be no further large crowds in the one-hundred and fifty-two-year-old church that he loved, but if it were to be so, this was the way to end it all, with an exodus to a new land. The drama of it ignited his oratory passion so that he felt he could walk on the water between the boats, lift them so that they floated on the wind instead of the sea. He inhaled with satisfaction. He barely knew what he would say. But he knew it would be spellbinding.

The sun lifted over the eastern land, the ocean rippling with the wind. The townspeople hugged and greeted each other and tried to joke, but the atmosphere was somber. This was the end of the town. This was the end of all they knew. Some were leaving sick loved-ones behind. There could be no real happiness here, but they sure tried to pretend there was.

Reg waved to them from the bow of the *Maggie Marie*, the boat he owned with his brother. That brother would remain behind, a sister-in-law near death, her brother not far behind. He had his nephew, a ten-year-old, who would soon be an orphan. His plan was to fish if he could get her licensed to do so in Quebec. Either way she was an asset even if he wound up selling her to start a new life for them all. Nobody knew quite what they would do beyond getting to the mainland of Canada. A whistle from RJ quietened the crowd.

"Psalm 107:23-31," Roy began. "Some went down to the sea in ships and plied their trade in deep waters;

They beheld the works of the Lord and His wonders in the deep. Then He spoke, and a stormy wind arose, which tossed high the waves of the sea. They mounted up to the heavens, and fell back to the depths, their hearts melted because of their peril. They reeled and staggered like drunkards and were at their wits' end. Then they cried to the Lord in their trouble, and He delivered them from their distress. He stilled the storm to whisper and quieted the waves of the sea. They were glad because of the calm, and He brought them to the harbour they were bound for. Let them give thanks to the Lord for His mercy and the wonders He does for His children."

It was quiet except for the engines, the occasional cough and the ocean dribbling between the wharf spans. It rolled in and receded and created the backdrop for Roy's speech.

"The mayor would like to say a few words. Jean?"

A quick squeeze of RJ's hand and she moved forward.

"Hello everyone." She hoped they could hear her." I don't speak as the mayor. I think such labels are unimportant at this point. Instead, I speak as your friend and neighbour. This community—you all—welcomed me, a come-from-away, and made me feel like I was one of you. You scoffed at my mainland ways, but in such a good-natured way that it felt like part of the welcome. I even got Max to eat guacamole." There was a general laugh, as they all poked fun at her strange food at first.

"Now we get to part ways under the worst of circumstances. Once I've got things settled here, I'll join you and I hope to see you on the other side. I wish you safe travels, smooth sailing—" her voice broke and she hesitated, breathing, trying to control emotion that swept like a wave, drowning her in its intensity.

"I can't," she breathed, her sobs coming in large gulps, her tears a collection that had formed when they first realized the severity of the situation. RJ came forward and held her. Several people around her sobbed as well.

"Yes, you can, my love," RJ whispered. "You have to buoy them up. They're counting on that."

One more deep breath. She lifted her head, wiped her eyes, and looked at the people, five boatloads of them, their eyes large and frightened, hearts beating with anxiety.

"I am going to miss you all, but I will see you over there in Quebec. I am sad, I'm not going to pretend that this town I adopted as mine won't always have a piece of my heart, but we will all be fine. We will all see each other and have a big reunion once we get to where we're going. Thank you for everything and as a final gift to you I promise not to sing the hymn that Roy has planned loudly enough for any of you to hear."

Her quip about her notoriously bad singing lightened the mood and laughter broke the string of tension that tethered them, taut, to their grief.

Roy reclaimed the service then, putting his oratory skills to great use, building on her speech impeccably, reassuring the crowd that community was a heart construct and that they would all be one community forever even if they were separated geographically.

"We are tied by our bond to this place, to Desolate Island, a bond that never can be severed. We will tell our children that this was home and how it was. How we sang and danced together, how we loved and cared for one another and how it was a special place with a unique culture. We will never forget, though we wander far." His hands waved, his voice boomed and those gathered were spellbound by his performance.

"Now let us sing the Mariner's hymn for the last time upon these shores. We will send you off as we have sent the fishers off in the past. But you go with the greatest fisher, Our Lord Jesus Christ, a fisher of men, and you will be floated across the gulf uneventfully and easily, and welcomed to that shore just as we, the people of God are welcomed on that celestial shore when we finish our final journey."

Then he opened his hymnal to the page he'd marked, though he, like most of the others, knew the old hymn off by heart.

"Eternal Father, strong to save, whose arm hath bound thy restless way..." He was joined by the other voices of those gathered, some loud and strong, some off key, others mouthing the words like Jean, their singing voices silenced by the insults driven deep into them in the past when they had sung loud enough to be heard. The breeze carried their lament across the water. The sun shone on flapping scarves and lowered heads.

"O Trinity of love and power, our brethren shield in danger's hour; from rock and tempest, fire and foe, protect them wheresoe'r they go; thus, evermore shall rise to thee glad hymns of praise from land and sea."

The Lord's Prayer was recited, and the ceremony ended with a loud Amen. The crowd didn't quite know what to do at that point and Jean too remained still, cheeks burnt with the brisk wind but unable to move, her hand held fast by Ashlyn's, and her back leaning against RJ who also stood immobile, waiting.

The boats were revved and one at a time they moved forward, The *Maggie Marie* in the lead followed by the

Grand Seafarer, the *Navigator's Dream*, the *Brandi Ryan* and the last of the five, the *Rae of Hope*.

Nearly all of those gathered left on the boats. A few stayed behind and sobbed while others stoically made their way home, wondering if they had made the right choice. They needed to see the vessels as they dropped over the horizon out of sight though they had to settle for the sharp cut around the point of the harbour, past Herring Head Rock and then out of view.

All of Jean's family, guests, and neighbours except for Mallory and Max walked the long road where RJ had proposed to Jean. Max had decided that if he didn't go to church in the good times, he wouldn't be heading there in the bad and that included services that were held outside. Mallory was afraid she would see Francis. Jean couldn't wait to tell her he was on Reg's boat, sullen but most definitely there. She was free.

Max waited at the door for them, the binoculars on his neck.

"They've cleared the head and are headed straight westerly," he informed them.

"They'll make it," Jean said. "I'm going to go around, see what the people left behind need before I go. Mallory, Francis is gone, I saw him on the *Maggie Marie*. We should go to your place, see what's left. See if there is anything you need."

"Is it right to be happy?" Mallory asked. She had her whole life ahead of her to live as she pleased. She couldn't wait to start it once they got to Quebec. She refused to think they wouldn't make it.

"It is always right to be happy," RJ answered, putting his arm around Jean's waist.

"RJ is right. I think, in the stress of all this, any happiness we can find we should grab."

"I'm happy," Ashlyn piped up. "I miss Mommy but I'm happy because I have a new mommy and a daddy. And I never had a daddy before in my entire life."

They all laughed. An entire life of three years. They could only hope she'd be given many more years of joy.

CHAPTER TWENTY-ONE

On board the American naval vessel *USS America*, Lieutenant Wasburg's hands shook, and his heart raced. The torpedoing and sinking of the Canadian Coast Guard vessel *CCGS James Bay* just off Labrador ended the unofficial ceasefire that had given them reprieve from the war. Things were in shambles as the naval battles escalated. Their communication system was down, with the last orders before they lost radio contact with their command being to destroy anything in the waters that moved.

"Captain, there are civilian vessels out there, we cannot obey this order," Lieutenant Gerald Wasburg pleaded with his superior officer.

"Lieutenant, until we regain communication the order stands. Any luck?"

"No, sir, the problem is not with us. It's out there." He nodded his head towards the open ocean. The satellites had been affected by a cyber attack yet again.

The ship's captain didn't know the full extent of the damage beyond what he heard from the American army soldiers they'd spoken to several days before. He'd promised the townspeople someone would come back but nobody would. Their contamination was too great for any chance of recovery and not wanting to lower the morale on his ship, he left them there, his own country's soldiers, with some food and an empty promise. He wasn't a cold-hearted man, but he had a job to do. And his job was to protect these waters from enemy attack, to prevent a further invasion of North America. Ships like his lined the eastern and western seaboards. They had not seen battle yet themselves, but they had seen its impact on land, their machines detecting the radiation that filtered through the air not far from them.

Lieutenant Wasburg had assured the residents of the little island of Desolate that it would be safe to leave. Now he could only hope that they decided not to. That hope was dashed when a blip in the radar was reported and the size of it determined it was a fleet of small vessels. They were headed north.

"The orders do not apply to civilian vessels sir, surely not. Those are fishing boats."

The captain's brow furrowed. "The order stands, Lieutenant. Go issue it." He spoke, his voice strong. They had not seen battle and he did not relish seeing it. But he wouldn't disobey the first order he'd been given since they'd taken a stance here to protect their ally from the enemy.

Lieutenant Wasburg saluted in acknowledgment, defeated. He considered his options. If he defied, someone else would capitulate. There was nothing to be done. Plus, thus far, the captain had kept them safe. He had to trust him. Nothing could be certain and what if they were small enemy boats? Who could tell in the chaos of war?

Shortly after, he gave an order that would send the first torpedoes out of the ship, aim perfect, their design a technological masterpiece of destruction.

Reg steered the *Maggie Marie* along, checking the chart.

The little boat felt sometimes as though it wanted to go in another direction, so used to heading off to the crab fields this time in the spring. Last year the fishermen had voted to leave their union, had banded in large numbers to form a new one and had lobbied and won the rights to larger quotas. It had increased his income and that of his crew significantly. What good was all that now, Reg wondered as he steamed along.

They'd head north and then, after passing through the Straight of Belle Isle, they'd head south, then eventually west. The limited amount of Cleanfuel had prevented them from making their way into the more populous areas of Quebec. The hope was they could purchase more there and then carry on along the coast. Reg thought though, perhaps he would try to return to a small town to fish. It was all to be determined after they docked. He hoped the weather held.

The waters were a gentle lop, no sea on, a few icebergs off in the distance. The boat felt heavy, its human cargo a weight on the vessel and on the mind.

The familiar red Coastguard boats hadn't been spotted this year at all. Normally they'd be scouring the shoreline, busy putting out buoys and doing what they always did, guard the coast. '

He felt safe as he guided the little fleet past the American ship.

"Look at that Layden, b'y, can't see the island anymore from this side of her," he said, impressed by its size.

"She's got planes on her. Never seen one take off yet though."

"No air war on right now, I suppose. But good to have her 'longside if we're attacked again," Reg mused.

"When do you figure we'll make land?"

"Good question. I'd like to know too." Francis struggled to stay upright though the wheelhouse barely moved.

"You looks a bit green around the gills there, b'y," Reg said, noting the pale skin and watery eyes of the man before him.

"You best get out on deck, don't be yuckin' yer guts up in here." Layden moved to open the door.

"I'm not sick. I don't get seasick. I just think you're going too slow. I've seen this boat go a lot faster than this when you take off in the spring."

"This is the speed we're going. Seven knots is average. We calculated the fuel, and we have to take our time. There is no rush."

"No rush? The waters might be swarming with U-boats. The Russians are everywhere. So's the Chinese."

"U-boats? Is this 1942? U-boats were the German subs ninety years ago. We would be lucky if there were some of those around. Germany is the only country we know that is on side with us. And the Americans. They'll keep these waters clear."

Reg kept his eyes straight ahead, Layden sat on a stool, a look of scorn on his face as he watched Francis' back when he opened the door to the outside and stepped onto a small strip that allowed passage from bow to aft. It was almost too narrow for the heavy-set man who leaned and hurled over the rail.

The wheelhouse door swung open and shut, banging. Layden closed it, leaving Francis on the other side.

Reg saw the black item in the water, thought it a whale or porpoise, its shadow to the starboard side but he was blown through the wheelhouse roof, neck broken, body splattered in pieces before it registered what it really was. Layden was in the middle of laughing at Francis throwing up over the side when he hit the wall. He managed a look of confusion before the life drained from his shattered body.

Francis and several others on the deck were thrown overboard, surviving the crash. Most of those who went into the water screamed until the cold stole their body heat and they perished in a short but agonizing period of time.

The boats behind them exploded like turrs picked off a rock. Bam. Bam. Bam. Bam.

Wood and bone splintered, fuel and blood mixed. The water ignited and combustion was immediate.

Some, like Raylene Pelley, lived long enough to make a choice no mother should have to make — to dive into the water with her two children to freeze or drown, or burn. She took their arms and jumped.

Most, the lucky ones, went into cold shock immediately, swallowed water and died in a few moments. But a few found items to float upon. Francis was one of these people. Surely the American ship could see what had happened. Surely, they would send rescue. The Russians or Chinese had done this, and the Americans would save them.

He died but not before realizing nobody was coming because it had been his heroes, the Americans, that had fired the explosives.

***

"Thunder in May?" Jean remarked, hearing a rumbling in the distance. She glanced out at the sky. No sign of a plane.

"Daresay, not like we can get a forecast out here these days," Mallory replied, bread lined across the table, its smell too much for Jean who grabbed a loaf, broke off a bun, and started to eat it.

"I'd kill for some butter," she said. They saved what they had for baking not spreading this past while.

"There wasn't even a tub of margarine left," Mallory announced. She'd gone to her old house to see what they could grab but there was nothing of any use.

"RJ, how is everybody?"

"Not good, fourteen more dead. I told Roy to go ahead and do the funerals kind of quiet like, but he wants to have a full church service. There's hardly anybody left to go mourn for God's sake." He picked up the binoculars out of habit, pointing them towards the American naval ship. There was a plume of smoke rising from beyond it. He opened the window. It stuck. He yanked at it, his patience thinning. The boys should be around that location now he figured. Then he smelled it. The wind was gentle but on the land. It was the odour of burning fuel. He closed the window.

"Anything wrong?" Jean asked, coming over, thinking that his taut face was troublesome.

"Oh no, thinking about the boys, I say they're making good time." No point in worrying Jean. He knew nothing for sure.

"How's the boat coming along?"

"She's ready, we can load up tonight, and leave right away."

"RJ, what is wrong?" She glanced at Mallory who sensed something also. "Tell us."

"Not a thing. Geez, my mind is full of stuff, it's not an easy thing you know, deciding to traipse around the Northern Pen and across the gulf."

Ashlyn walked in, saw him, picked up speed, and launched herself into his arms. She was bathed and powdered and smelled like roses. She deserved a chance at life, and he hoped to provide it. There was nothing here but dying and death. Ashlyn deserved life and he'd do his damnedest to give it to her.

"Are we going out on the big boat soon?"

"Yes, my love, in a few hours. You're all bathed and dressed for it, I see. Those your sailing clothes?"

"Yep, Daddy, I'm ready. Know what, Daddy, I was thinking."

"What, dolly?" He loved her tiny little voice calling him 'Daddy'.

"We're like the piners."

"The piners? What are the piners?"

"You know, the piners. Mommy, my other mommy, used to read me *Little House on the Prairie* and they were piners. They moved out and settled in a new place. We're the same, we're moving to settle in a new place. We're piners and if they can be brave and face what they don't know then I can be too. I can be a brave piner like Laura."

"You are a very wise girl," Jean said, her smile wide.

"I think you mean pioneers, sweetie," RJ said. "You are very right. We are pioneers, and we will be very brave. You're very smart, you know."

She hugged his neck. Jean ruffled her hair and Mallory stepped back, packing the bread in bags for the journey.

RJ didn't feel so brave. They had agreed on radio silence until they were both on the other side, their paranoia at being spotted alone and vulnerable on the water now stealing the only way he would have had to contact them.

He was worried. Jean sensed it was over far more than the trip, but she didn't want to know. She was exhausted from knowledge and ready to lay her fate in the hands of somebody else for a while. So she didn't ask, and he didn't volunteer. They continued preparing to leave. It was a sad task but one that kept her mind off those who had already gone. They had to be alright, she thought. But she had a funny feeling in her gut that perhaps they weren't.

CHAPTER TWENTY-TWO

Desolate Island had always been a quiet place. Now though, the silence was haunting. There were no songbirds, no gulls squawking, and not even the sea made noise this calm evening. The boat loaded, RJ tucked Ashlyn into one of the bunks, covered her up, snuggled a few toys in and kissed her cheek. Mallory would share with her. RJ and Jean would stay awake all the first night navigating. Max and Ralph would take over the second shift tomorrow. It should only take a few days if the weather remained calm. The neighbours were not navigators, so they would cook and take watches if required, the hold converted to sleeping area for them all as they left the island they loved so much.

Desolate Island. A misnomer. Historical papers gave evidence the town had been named the far more appropriate *île du Soleil* by its original French settlers. Island of Sun. It had been bastardized by the English into Desolate Island. There had never been anything desolate about it, but its name, until recently.

Back at the house, Jean and RJ took a last walk around.

A hollow feeling sat in Jean's chest when it came time to say a final goodbye. It spread itself throughout her entire body, an ache that stripped her ability to cry. It was a harbinger of despair. It cried a desperate refrain. *I don't want to go.*

"I thought when the lights went out, it was a breaker," Jean said, her hand running over the panel box, the glow of the kerosene lantern illuminating the room. "Then, I thought it was due to the storm although the storm had ended the night before. That was what I thought but something in me knew it wasn't either of those things. It was like my brain was full of ideas and possibilities, but my heart was full of dread and despair."

"I thought what a waste my life had been," RJ said. "And then I thought, what a waste it would have been anyway. There are forty-three people left alive on this island right now. And after we leave there'll be thirty something, all dying except the minister, but he's dying too, just not actively sick. It's all a waste. We spent hours and hours fighting DFO for that crab quota last year. We were so happy when we won. All that time battling, and I could have been playing guitar or singing. Or playing cards with Dad."

"We have to eat so we fight for that." The room was empty without Jean's large avocado trees that were in the hold of the boat. She had worked so hard to get them to grow, she couldn't leave them behind. She'd left her journals. She knew that they would paint a picture of life on Desolate Island that future explorers might appreciate and that if anything ever could bring her back, it would be that.

"We weren't fighting to eat. That was a big lie. We were fighting so we could make payments on bigger boats, so we could buy bigger houses, cars, trucks. I was so frustrated that Dad wanted to keep his old boat, not go invest in a bigger one, hire a crew, make more money. It was all so foolish. Four or five people dying a day now, Jean. For the past while it's been nothing but death. It's hard to see the point after that."

"If there is a purpose to life, I don't know it, RJ. But we do cling on to it, so there must be one. We'll see what's left of our people when we get to Quebec. I suppose we just have to be happy, look forward to that."

He breathed deep, the instinct to tell her his suspicions battling with his need to keep her from worrying. It served no purpose and perhaps he was wrong. He remained silent.

"It doesn't matter what you do, Jean, we all end up in the same place. We can be alive here, we can be alive as we steam across the water, we can be alive in a Quebec town, or we can be dead in all these places. There's no difference. We are either alive or dead."

"I don't think life is about living and dying," Jean said. "It's about time and your use of it. Life isn't something you're given or something you must do a certain way, it's a speck of opportunity to live in awareness and to have consciousness for a while. It's not a substance to be moulded into a thing, it has no matter, no form, it has no reason or purpose, it just is. This moment, nobody has lived before. But you and I are here, witnesses, the only ones in it. And we have control over what we make of it."

Her hands moved as she spoke, punctuating her words.

"Well, I choose to make this of it," he said, reaching out for her, pulling her close, meeting her lips.

They were ghosts. Shadows on the wall created by the flicker of the kerosene lamp, its oily smell wafting in the empty room. They could have taken more time. But they only took what was required.

The door closed behind them. Jean left it unlocked, the keys on the table in case one day a wanderer required shelter. As they headed towards the dock, a voice called out. It came from behind the small store that had once held fishing gear but now held Jean's patio furniture.

"You're leaving now? Tonight? May I come with you?" It was Roy Pearcey, the light of the lantern revealed when Jean held it aloft.

"Yes, how did you know?" RJ asked.

"I didn't, but I took a chance. They're all sick. Everyone of them. I don't want to be the only survivor here once they're all gone. I know, as the minister I should stay but—" His eyes cast down, his height diminished, his foot kicked at a stone.

"Is that all you have?" RJ indicated the case in his hand.

"A bit more. My Bible and robe and some clothes just back there."

"What about Rufus?"

The small dog came at his name, he had been sniffing around the ground, his beagle nose always at work.

"If he can't come, I'll leave him. But I do have a plastic crate I always kept him in."

"No, he can come, right, Jean?" RJ bent down and petted the dog.

"Well, the cats aren't going to be happy but they're in a crate anyway too. You'll have to take him on deck for business and clean up after him. Otherwise, of course you can."

"Yes, yes for sure. Thank you, my friends." The boom of preaching had left his voice. It was meek and grateful.

He smiled at RJ. They had gone to school together, been good buddies as boys, but he'd gone religious, and RJ had gone away.

"Let's go," Jean said, leading them towards the boat, its lights a strange yellow in the pitch-black sky, electric illumination almost alien now.

Jean took the beagle to the galley, while the men shoved off from the dock. The boat's engines roared into a higher gear. Roy would have to sit at the table and make the best of it. All the bunks were full. He'd sleep somewhere at some point, but right now everybody except Ashlyn seemed wide awake, nerves taut like the ropes that had tethered the small longliner to the wharf moments before.

RJ was at the wheel and his father read paper navigation charts beside him as they cruised along.

Jean looked out, the night sky a shroud of stars. But before them there was only black water. She'd have to trust the fishermen to know the way, they'd plotted and planned the trip for days. She didn't want to be like a child asking, how much farther, but RJ spoke anyway. His words shocked her.

"We've decided to go another route," he informed her. "it'll take longer but we've plenty of fuel onboard. I seems Dad's hoarding finally came in handy."

Ralph Sr. grinned.

"After all that planning, why?" Jean asked. "We are supposed to meet the others. They'll be concerned if we —"

"I feel like it's better if, after we're over in the gulf, we sail further south, then cross into Quebec, instead of going across and then down. Max agrees." He didn't tell her that if they hugged the coastline, they might also stay out of radar or firing range of the American ship, or any others that might be nearby. He also didn't tell her that Max had had a premonition.

"I guess I better learn to trust your feelings, uh? Who knew you were so intuitive?" she said, pulling herself up into a tall stool and peering ahead into the night. Perhaps there was something to look forward to. Her last new beginning had been good. She'd make the most of this one too.

They *were* piners, she thought with an amused grin at the memory of Ashlyn's story. A wave of nausea struck. She sucked in a deep breath, smiled, jumped up and walked out of the wheelhouse onto the deck where she relieved her stomach over the rail. After five or six minutes, shivering, legs weak, she made her way back inside.

"Seasick?" RJ asked her. Dear Lord, he hoped that's what it was. If she had the sickness, they had left too late. Nobody so far had survived it.

"Yeah," she lied, her thoughts similar to his. That's what it had to be. She settled back down in the chair, worrying her lip with her teeth, staring, unseeing out the wheelhouse windows.

She had never been seasick a day in her life.

CHAPTER TWENTY-THREE

The ocean swells lifted the boat up, setting it down with a thud, repeating the motion until Jean was exhausted from the effort of keeping herself upon the chair.

Every inch of her screamed to escape, turn around, go back, the dark a close and cold place, a grave. She felt buried alive in the dimly lit wheelhouse, at the mercy of the ocean and the man at the wheel, in the middle of the darkest of nights.

RJ hadn't spoken for a while, deep in his thoughts, directing the little boat over the swells, doing his job, being a sailor like the vast majority of those who lived on the shores left behind.

"How will we communicate to the others?" Jean asked.

"What?" RJ looked at her, then back out the window.

"To tell them we're going in a totally different direction."

"Jean..." Her name dropped, heavy, grave. It weighed him down, held him firm to the floor. Hands on the wheel, he searched out the window, eyes scanning beyond the bow of the boat as though the right words were out there, suspended in the dark.

"What? RJ?" Her heart jumped, filled her chest. She

felt the weight too, heavy like the ballast set in the hold of a boat to keep her balanced in her buoyancy.

"I don't think they made it, Jean. I saw smoke from behind the Navy ship. I can't say for certain, but it was right when they would have gone past her. That's why we're going this way, tighter to shore." The right words didn't exist. Never had. There were only ordinary words, their meaning filled with horror.

"Oh my God, no. Why didn't you tell me?"

"I couldn't be sure, and I didn't want to worry you. What would be the point?"

"Dear Lord, all of them? Gone? RJ? I can't even think about it. There were children." Her mind flew to Ashlyn, sound asleep in the bunk. She loved her fiercely, as one loves something they didn't know they wanted until it was gifted to them. She was her child, tiny hands made to be held by hers, the soft downy hair on her head created for her strokes at night.

"I can't be sure." But he was. He had seen some debris. Not much, the wind was off the land for quite a while again now. But it had veered and strengthened, and some things had floated ashore, defiant. Strips of wood, fiberglass slivered to kindling, with blue paint like that of the *Maggie Marie*. A small suitcase that he was sure Francis carried. But he hadn't looked closer, had avoided looking at the water while there was still daylight, avoiding seeing anything more than that which showed itself while he prepared for their escape.

"You saw something, didn't you? You know, don't you?"

"Yeah, I know." The admission brought an ache to his eyes. He needed to get them to their destination and couldn't think about this.

Jean's eyes filled. She stood, wobbly on the heaving floor. She wrapped her arms around his waist from behind, not moving. Just holding him there.

"What caused it, RJ? Are there Russians?"

"Jean, I think it was the Americans."

"The Americans? They wouldn't do that. They were the ones that told us to leave. They said it was safe."

"I see no signs of other vessels. If there was an enemy ship that destroyed the longliners, don't you think the Americans would be defending it? Don't you think they would have sent tenders out to save who they could? Come warn us? It's the American Navy, Jean. Plus, I think they did it. I don't know why but I do."

"Oh my God, are they the enemy now?"

"This war is so crazy, how are we supposed to know? It sounds like every atomic bomb ever made has been dropped. Jean, I can't be sure what we'll find when we reach the mainland. Quebec is a major city, Montreal, who knows at this point. If the rest of Canada isn't hit, perhaps everybody is going there like everybody has always gone there. We've been cut off for so long."

"What about the radio?"

"I am going to make contact when we're close to the shore. If I can. We have a long trip ahead of us yet."

"Maybe we should go to Corner Brook?"

"I think this province is a write-off Jean, you know that. We discussed it. We were in bad enough shape before but now there's no recovery from this mess. I think our best option is to make our way to the mainland."

"I know, I know, you think it's a waste of time to spend time in this province when we could be building a new life elsewhere, and I know it makes sense, it's just that...it's so far to go. And in these waters."

"Gulf ferries aren't running, you know?"

"How do you know that?"

"I've had a few two-way radio conversations. Nobody is talking so it's hard to reach but I've managed to reach a couple people. There is a fuel shortage, crew shortage, crew members that were home when the bombs hit. Too bad they never finished that tunnel across the straights. Bloody short-sighted politicians."

"What else do you know? Do you know how many were killed? In the bombing?"

He glanced at her, then decided to tell her. She wasn't somebody who needed protecting. He only kept the information quiet to process it himself. Now he was ready to talk about it.

"The numbers keep changing. Fifty thousand, seventy thousand, a hundred thousand."

"Fifty thousand is the lowest number you heard? Damn." Her mind had an easier time grasping the breadth of the ocean than those numbers.

"We simply don't know. There truly isn't news anymore, the news people were in the centers that were hit, remember, so we just don't know. Something has happened in the gulf too. Shipping traffic has pretty much come to a halt, I don't know why, nobody knows why. They said a Canadian Coast Guard ship was blown up near Port au Choix but somebody else said they heard it was up near Labrador. The Canadian navy is around here somewhere but it's bad out there." He nodded at the ocean before him. "The world is a dark place. I don't know how you ever get used to the dark." He started straight ahead, Jean's embrace keeping him upright. He was supposed to wake somebody for a shift eventually, but he doubted he would sleep until he had them safely through the straits at least.

RJ and Jean steamed all night and the next day they did sleep, despite RJ's suspicion that he wouldn't be able to. Max and Ralph navigated the daylight hours without incident. They handed off the wheel the second night and were about three hours into it, now heading across the gulf towards Quebec.

Jean looked out at the rising waters, blackened by the drizzle that started right after they took over. She could tell the water from the sky, but it was still ink-black, the horizon a thin band of ebony in the distance. "You get used to everything over time, don't you? When the power went out first, I kept hitting switches out of habit. I haven't hit a switch in months now. When you started up the longliner, all the lights running it felt too bright, harsh, artificial. It took my eyes a while to get used to the light after so little for so long, but I did. Now I can see the water, but an hour ago all I could see was a black wall of nothing. So, I suppose we'll get used to this new, darker world. Try to bring some light into it if we live."

"We were pretty spoiled before," RJ answered. "I used to grumble to Dad that we needed a new truck, an electric one like most people have. I was embarrassed to be driving around in that old rusty Chev of his. And then, we had no fuel to run the thing and there were days I craved to be able to just jump aboard it. But we had no electricity either, so what good would that new electric have been?"

"Nothing mattered that I thought mattered. I remember stressing about the slow internet speed because I couldn't activate Holo. And what a crazy amount of time I wasted watching cat videos for God's sakes."

"Cat videos were not a waste of time. I hope Tomcat can't hear you," he joked. "Yeah, we took it all for granted. I know I did. Remember those, *we got to take care of our own people first*, types. Now we're those people, needing taking care of. Funny how this war had nothing to do with terrorists, remember back when that was the big fear? They weren't the big threat after all, they didn't have the nuclear weapons, we did. Well, the west, not Canada."

"What is that smell, RJ?" Jean asked, changing the subject.

He raised his nose, sniffed. "I don't know, oil of some kind. Maybe I have a leak."

"I think it's outside?" Jean left RJ and went to the side door. She opened it and the cold air hit her face and chilled the wheelhouse in an instant. She battled the wind to keep it open. A strong, petroleum odour floated on the night breeze.

"Let me go, just hold the wheel, keep her dead ahead, I'll go check." How could they be leaking fuel? It was nearly impossible, RJ thought.

Jean brought the door towards her with a bang and went to take over the wheel. RJ geared up for the cold, then went outside, the door closing fast beside him. She focused on holding the tiny boat steady as she punched through the water, straight ahead. She swore she could see the glow of the lights from a ship or land in the distance. But just when she was sure, it vanished. Perhaps she was like a desert traveler, so desperate for water she was seeing a mirage.

RJ came back in a short while later, something in his hands.

"What is it?" she asked, eyeing the long piece of wood he held in his hand.

"Nothing good," he said, holding the stick out to her.

"Where did that come from?" she asked, realizing what it was he held in his hand.

"I've no idea but looks like we're not out here completely alone after all."

CHAPTER TWENTY-FOUR

"I'd say something hit a ship. It's all over, we're steaming through it, the boat is covered with this. It is sticking to the sides. I don't say it'll ever come off." RJ pointed to the thick gunk on the plank.

"Could a ship have started leaking?" Jean stared out at the ocean as though it held the answer.

"I don't know. All I know is that it's an oil product, doesn't matter what kind. Jeez, we're in a bloody minefield out here."

"So, what does that mean? For us. Can we steam through it? Will it cause problems? Who the hell is blowing up ships?" Jean's heart plummeted. She'd allowed herself to believe they'd be safe. Odds were against that, and this brought the reality of their plight slam bang into her consciousness again.

"Other ships, submarines I daresay, and I don't know that we have much choice but to keep steaming. We'll be going in blind, but we gotta go. I think it'll be on the surface so it shouldn't affect us that much but it's going to stink and we're going to be breathing it. It's not good. But I don't see that we have much choice."

"Oh God. Maybe keep everybody downstairs? Find something to wear as a mask to filter it a bit?" Jean wrinkled her nose. "We have those old Covid masks in the cupboard." They'd kept a stock on hand after the second pandemic of 2028 although that hadn't been as bad as 2020. All masks were called Covid masks, even though that had ended twenty plus years ago, with the second being a new influenza strain.

"I think that's a good idea. But let's not tell them yet, see how it goes," RJ said, glancing at the stick with the glob of tar.

"Okay. We'll only scare them." Jean felt light-headed along with the constant nausea. The oil wasn't bothering her much.

"Jean, I have a question. It may be strange that we never talked about this before but how old are you? You're obviously not old enough to be retired."

"You're trying to distract me, right? Or the fumes got to you already? Okay, I'll play. I'm forty-one. This is a strange conversation to be having right now you know."

"I've learned recently that if you think of a conversation to have—you best have it because you may not get another chance."

"Too true, so, how old are you?"

"Thirty-three."

"I feel like a cradle robber now." She grinned.

"Cougar! Seriously though, it's not that much difference."

"I know. I retired at thirty-one."

"That's crazy. How did you manage that?"

"I ran my own e-commerce company for eight years, Jadler Corporation. We created a specialized AI technology, then sold it to A-Zon. I made a small fortune and retired." She made it sound easy, but she had nearly burnt out in that decade, her retirement a last-ditch effort to survive, her move to Desolate Island a rejection of her old life-style. She didn't recognize the crazy, driven woman she had been back then. She'd rejected all but the most basic technology which was odd considering her background. She fit in with the rest of the province in that way.

"It's very odd to have these normal, domestic conversations while we're steaming through an oil spill on our way to try to start a new life after a nuclear winter in our home province." Jean shook her head and laughed.

RJ joined in her mirth. "Humans are strangely adaptive creatures."

"Oh, while you were out on the deck, I think I saw lights ahead. I'm not sure what they are."

"I don't see anything." He grabbed the binoculars. He glanced into the radar, there was a blip ahead, not too far. "Yeah, there's something out there."

"How far away?"

"It's almost dead ahead of us, we'll come upon it soon."

"Should we detour?"

"I don't think there's any point. I think we need to go straight ahead and take things as they come. There's no strategy out here. We could turn and run into a worse situation."

Jean knew he was right but damn. It all seemed so dangerous.

"Shit, whatever it is, it's on fire." He could see the glow of flame ahead. He could smell smoke too.

"What? Here, take the wheel." She grabbed the binoculars in one hand and looked until he took over. There were several fires, the oil on the water burned in places but a central flame was where she focused her attention.

"It's a ship on fire, RJ, and there's fire in places all

around. Dear Lord, what do we do?"

"We keep on going. Go through it. That's where the oil came from that we're steaming through."

"We could catch on fire, couldn't we?"

"We could but I don't see any way around it plus it might even be safer. If this ship was blown up nobody would expect another to steam through the debris unless they had to. Nobody's watching a destroyed ship."

"I didn't even think of that."

"Is everybody sleeping? Go check. I want Ashlyn asleep. Give her something if you have to." They had already discussed that they would make sure that if the worst occurred and if there was time, they would ensure the child was unaware, should they be in imminent danger.

Mallory had raided her medicine cabinets at the inn after the others had left and pulled Ativan and Valium, among other pills, out of there. They were tucked in an emergency first aid box stored in one of the cupboards.

Jean slipped into the galley. She pulled a tiny white pill out of the box, crushed it and put it into a spoonful of jam. Max stirred, but she shushed him and told him to go back to sleep. She indicated to Ralph that he should go up however and Max, being Max went too, despite her admonishment.

Mallory awakened, there was no choice but to disturb her to get to the child.

"We're coming upon a wreck, just in case, we want Ashlyn to sleep through it." Mallory took the spoon and nodded. She lifted the child who was warm and malleable in her slumber. She whispered, "Eat this, it's like candy," into her ear. And the child opened her eyes, smiled then allowed herself to be fed.

"Go back to sleep now, sweetie. I'll be up as soon as I know she's sound," Mallory whispered to Jean who nodded. They didn't need all hands-on-deck, but they needed more than they had.

She went up to the wheelhouse, nodded to Ralph who gave a subtle acknowledging nod of his own. He wore a one-piece survival suit, dressed for the deck. He had the gear for these conditions. He was going to the bow to watch for whatever needed to be watched. He tied an old shirt around his face, while the rest put on the disposable masks Jean had mentioned before. He opened the door and with a breeze through the wheelhouse, he was gone.

RJ flicked on the exterior lights, illuminating the area around them. They'd been running dark to avoid detection but needed lights now to navigate. Thick plumes of smoke rose from the water, but the oil was not on fire itself.

"Whatever this is, it doesn't combust easy," RJ said. "Probably that new, so-called Pure-fuel. We best get through as fast as we can." He increased the speed, pushed through the ocean heavy with the strange petroleum. The air was nearly as thick as the water, the pungent odour penetrating the walls of the wheelhouse. There was less smoke port, so RJ steered them left but avoiding debris was more difficult, so he slowed back down again, going starboard. He kept his eye on his father who was watching for anything that might damage the hull if he struck it.

When Ralph Senior raised his arm, in a gesture that said there's something ahead, Jean pulled the hood tight on her parka and went to join him, the wind batting her in the facial skin that was exposed around the mask.

"What's the trouble, Ralph?" she asked.

The shy man, who hated talking to women, had no

choice but to answer. His voice cracked under his nervousness, a strange affliction in a place where fire was the greater threat.

"There's bodies." He gestured to the water and Jean looked where he pointed.

"Oh my God." She put her hand over her mouth as they steamed past them, two men, frozen in death, their eyes open to the dark sky.

"That one's burned," Ralph pointed to another, face down this time atop a piece of debris, his clothing blackened, skin melted to the fibers. The thick air impaired their breathing, flames crackling to the starboard as the boat made its way through the dark, thick water. More bodies littered the surface. A sharp whistle brought Ralph's head upright. He shaded his hand over his eyes as though to block out the sun.

"You heard that too?"

"Yes, over to the port." He pointed then, looking back at the wheelhouse, giving direction to RJ who seemed to know exactly what his father meant. The boat veered a little.

"Do you see anything?"

"There, on the water. Go tell RJ to slow down. Somebody's alive out there."

Jean stumbled along, her feet slipping on the slick deck, making her way to the wheelhouse.

"There's somebody in the water. Follow your father's directions."

"Holy jeez, are you sure?" Mallory, masked and now up in the wheelhouse, asked.

"Yeah, we got to save whoever it is."

"Yes, we do," Max repeated. He looked ready to head out on deck to help.

"Max you stay in here, we'll go out and help."

"I'm coming, I needs to be at something."

Jean nodded, she understood. He walked out, steady for an old guy. She shook her head, stubborn old geezer.

"I'm going to slow down to a crawl, Dad is saying we're close. Go help him. Tie yourselves on if you have to if it gets too crazy out there."

The three of them made their way out to the door in time to hear the quietest man they'd ever known, Ralph Senior, shouting into the water.

CHAPTER TWENTY-FIVE

RJ maneuvered the boat as best he could. He aimed for the man, then brought her to a standstill, pulled in and knocked against the debris that kept the survivor out of the water and had saved his life.

Ralph leaned over, and reached for the man, grabbing his hand while the others held on to him, but he was too weak.

Ralph's suit had a deck safety harness, so he tethered himself on to the ring and leapt forward, sure-footed. He landed on the platform that the injured man floated upon. He couldn't identify it, but it was buoyant and the perfect makeshift life raft. He grabbed him underneath his armpits and made his way back. Those on deck pulled the rope forward, reached out, and grabbed for the man. Their hands yanked together. The weight pulled them towards the edge, but they clung on. Fumes filled their lungs, even through the masks, and they coughed, lifting them up over their faces to adjust them. They then pulled again until he slid on to the deck. They got Ralph in after, reaching for him as he leapt back onto the boat.

The rescued man still held the whistle clamped between his teeth, but he was aware. His blue lips trembled, and his survival suit was covered in thick oil. It smeared along the deck and left a black trail as they pulled him to the wheelhouse. Mallory went ahead, Max held the door, and the others hauled him inside as RJ revved up the engine. Ralph stayed on watch duty, a wave from him telling RJ when to go again. They would trudge on through, in the hope that fresh air waited for them not far ahead. Meanwhile they'd also watch for other survivors.

Mallory returned, first aid kit, towels, and blanket in her arms.

"Let's get him stripped down here and keep that suit, it might be full of oil but it's worth something I imagine," she instructed.

"Wake Colin down in the hold and tell him to give us a hand." Jean was glad that the nurse was on board. It reassured her.

"Already done, he's getting dressed." Max had intuited what was needed before they even knew what it was.

Mallory rubbed the man's hands, tried to get him to speak.

Moments later, Colin came through the door.

Max sat on the stool Jean had occupied earlier, watching the scene unfold. He felt funny, the smell of the oil making him sick, a strange weight on his chest impairing his breathing. He needed to rest a bit. He took the mask off his face and leaned back. He hated the damned things. Always had. He had raged against them in 2020, but in 2028 hindsight had realized how awful that was. It was, after all, no big deal to wear one, and it worked.

The young man they'd hauled aboard shivered when they removed the survival suit that revealed only pajama bottoms. He'd been smart enough not to waste time getting dressed when he'd felt the explosion, choosing instead to don the red immersion suit that was a twin to the one Ralph wore.

"Where do you hurt? Are you in any pain?" Colin asked, pressing this place and that, trying to assess the injuries.

"Just so tired," the man answered, and the room got considerably louder at the sound of his voice as they all started asking them questions.

"Shhh, quiet, everyone. Tell me, what happened?" RJ glanced back for a moment. Perhaps this guy could help him understand what they were facing.

"They're blowing up everything that moves," he said. His eyes filled.

"What's your name?" Colin asked again, irritated that RJ was interrogating this patient, his training embedded such that his patient came first. He tucked blankets around him and shot RJ a look.

"It's Adam Bayfield sir. I was on *The Medea*. That's what is on fire. We were struck, blown up. Everything is getting blown up. Don't you have the radio on?" His voice was stronger now, his exhaustion waning a little with the blankets being wrapped around him and the water they were giving him.

"We can't get anybody on any of the radios."

"It's hit or miss. We have a special frequency with our company." Adam coughed.

"We don't have any room in the galley to let you lay down. But we'll try to make you comfortable here."

"Put the young man in my bunk, Colin. RJ, steam straight through until you get there. Don't slow down for nothing. That's what you have to do," Max said.

RJ met his eyes and nodded. "If you say so. But you should probably lay down yourself."

Max didn't look well, RJ thought. The old guy had

been inhaling these fumes like the rest of them, but they weren't in their eighties. Max nodded, a smile on his face like he was going nowhere.

"So, you've no broken bones, no real injuries. I think we should get you to bed." Colin's assessment was complete.

"Not until I get some more information. I think I'll keep the radios off. I don't want to let on that we're here," RJ said. That too had been Max's suggestion. While he felt out of touch with the outside world, he trusted Max completely but still, information was power.

"Who is blowing everything up? Is there an active battle here?"

"Yes. It started when a Canadian Coastguard ship was hit. From what I understand, somebody is about to attack the coast of Canada, but nobody outside the military seems to know if it's the Russians or the Chinese or what. We were hit by the Americans."

"What the hell? The Americans blew up a cargo ship? What were you carrying? Stuff for the war?"

"We had steel. We weren't supposed to come through this route but were redirected because things are so bad. But it looks like it's bad all over."

"So, we're not at war with the Americans? Is *The Medea* a Canadian boat?"

"No, it's American."

"So, you think she was blown up by your own country?"

"I don't think so. I don't know." His eyes filled, and Jean couldn't decide if he was upset over what he'd been through or that it might have been caused by his own country.

"I don't think your guys did this," Jean said. She had

no idea if any of what she said was true, but she said it anyway. "And I know they didn't blow up the Coastguard. They're protecting North America, not at war with it. Mistakes happen, but Adam, most likely you were attacked by somebody else and that your navy will get whoever did this at some point. We're headed for Quebec, and we'll make sure to report the destruction of *The Medea*. Is your family safe? Where are you from?"

"Oh yes, thank you. I think I'm confused. No... my own country wouldn't attack its own ship? It wouldn't do that right? My family is in Wisconsin. It's fine there. Nobody's wasting bombs on them."

"Well, let's work on getting you back to them. We'll put you down in Max's bunk. Are you finished, RJ?" Jean asked.

"Yes," RJ said. "Thank you, Adam. I'm sorry to ask so much but I'm responsible to take us through and well, I need to know what we're facing. Do you think there is anything I should watch for?"

"I think you should get to land as quick as you can, get us to Quebec. I don't think you can do much more than that."

The wheelhouse got quiet when Mallory and Collin left, helping the young man down the stairs. They heard their voices, muffled behind the door. Jean stood by RJ, warm in the wheelhouse once the door could stay closed for a while. They had been moving forward and now were clear of the wreckage.

"Somebody should give your father a break," she commented.

"He won't leave that spot now." RJ watched his father on his belly at the bow, face forward, watching the water.

"Tough guy, do you think he'll spot more people?"

Jean was the opposite, looking away from the water, not wanting to see. "They don't make men like they did in your day, uh Max?"

She turned to the old guy, who had been quiet in the chair for a while. His eyes were closed, his body slumped down in the stool, arms resting on either side.

Jean smiled thinking he was like Ashlyn who could fall asleep anywhere if she didn't get to bed on time. She glanced at him again, his stillness unnatural, his position not one most could sleep in no matter how exhausted.

She walked over and touched his face. Her fingers grazed his cold skin. Her sharp intake of breath caused RJ to look around.

"I think Max is gone," she whispered. Her hand stroked his face again, then her fingertips made their way to his neck to search for a familiar throb. She found it absent. She pulled him up, then lowered him to the floor. She checked again and decided against getting Colin back. It was too late.

"What? No." RJ turned and looked at Max now prone on the floor behind him. He looked back to the front.

"Yeah, he's definitely gone. Oh my God. I can't believe it." Her tears washed her cheeks and dripped onto Max's face.

RJ slammed his hand on the wheel and shook his head. Then he bowed low. He felt the tears in his eyes and allowed the full sobs that welled up to escape. His breath caught, his years of disciplined control on his feelings a wasted practice.

"Oh sweetheart." Jean rose and went to him, her own grief matching his.

"It's too much, it's too damned much," he said, trying to rein in his emotions, to explain them. He failed at both.

"Yeah, it is. But Max was old, and he did so much, he had a good life."

"Know what he told me?" RJ asked. "He said he saw this all coming. That he knew from his grandfather's stories of the second world war that Newfoundland was a target. He told me he expected it any day. That the *Caribou* was torpedoed by the Germans in the gulf in World War II, that we're the front line if somebody wants to invade North America. He was totally opposed to letting the Americans set up here."

"Lots of people are saying that now."

"He told me that two years before all of this started. He told me he had dreams of a Navy boat off Desolate Island, that he saw soldiers coming ashore. He told me that he wouldn't live to the end of this war. It was very spooky that it all came to be."

"Wow, and that's exactly what happened."

"He was the one who told me to come this way, told me to leave alone and not with the others. My intuition was always his. I figured if he was right about the rest, it was best to go along. He's the seventh son of a seventh son. They got a gift, so they say. I never believed all this nonsense, but he predicted everything. Didn't he tell you his predictions? Now he's gone. What do we do now? I don't know what to do."

"He told me local stuff, but I thought he just knew everybody super well. What did he tell you to do? Did he give you advice?"

RJ took a deep breath. He glanced at the still body of his friend and mentor. Having Max to follow had not only provided direction, but it also took the responsibility off RJ. He would never say it out loud that this was the biggest reason for his breakdown. Now he was truly the one to blame if they didn't make it.

"He told me the same as the American guy did, to go straight though, non-stop until we reach land. He said if we got to Quebec and didn't go back to sea again, we'd all make it."

"Then that's what we do." Jean slipped away, heading to the galley to get Colin and Mallory. It was too late to save Max, but they needed the nurse to declare him dead. They needed to wrap him in something, lay him out on the deck. She would record his death in the log she kept. She still felt the pull of leadership, of record keeping. She didn't know why but the registering of death seemed very important.

One man rescued, another gone, Jean thought. This new day not even started, their voyage in its early hours, their route decided at the whims of a man now dead. Jean could hardly process it all.

RJ checked his equipment, his course set straight for Anticosti Island, but he wouldn't stop there but carry on past it, the entire island a hazard to approach without intimate knowledge of its rocky shores.

They had been at sea for just a few days. Another twenty-four, perhaps less if the weather held, should have them docked at Sept Illes.

Until then he had one job, to steer his boat straight on through. He'd have to do it despite his grief. And do it he would. Because everybody he loved depended on it.

CHAPTER TWENTY-SIX

The *June Delight* pulled into the port at Sept Iles on June 4, 2047 after a very slow trip. They had ridden out a short storm that had set them back and they watched carefully for enemy ships, or even friendly ones. Max laid wrapped in a tarp on the deck, preserved by the cold ocean temperatures that had dropped to near zero but felt even colder due to a sharp wind that rose up and greeted the tar-encrusted fishing boat.

All but RJ stood on the deck including the American, Adam, who now wore some of Max's clothes to keep warm. Jean's eyes scanned the scene as they made their way in. Ships pulled in and out, past the archipelago of islands that gave the region its name. RJ brought the tiny boat, dwarfed by some of the large vessels, towards the shore.

As they got closer Jean could see signs of electricity everywhere.

She pulled the A-Tab from the waterproof pouch, hit the power button, eyes glued to the upper right-hand corner for signs of a signal. It startled her when it pinged, and didn't stop, notifications from all who had tried to reach her since the war, arriving all at once.

"Oh my God, it works." Jean held the phone close to

her heart and wept, then scolded herself for the silliness. She'd survived, that should be the greater success but somehow, the little red notifications on her smart phone were a trigger and she broke down, strength gone. Mallory came to stand by her, Ashlyn held her hand tighter, and the others wore a combination of somber and worried expressions. What if they turned on their phones to hear bad news?

"There is still Facebook," she laughed. "And Twitter." But it was texts that she was most interested in. She replied to a frantic collection of them from her only living relative, her Aunt Amelia in Toronto. She asked her to let everyone know she was alive and in Quebec. Her immediate reply was an invitation to come to them. Relieved that indeed, Toronto still existed, she replied that they would talk later, after they docked. She now had a husband, a daughter, and a boat load of family to see to.

She scrolled through, replying with a quick, "I'm ok, will talk to you later," to the various friends who had checked on her.

She clicked on her Facebook messages, scrolled down, unable to believe there was data and that she was connected. So much for the satellites and towers all being destroyed. Truth, as they say, really was the first casualty of war.

She noticed a new friend request and clicked on it. She recognized the name. Her heart dropped as she clicked a yes and then a message appeared in her instant messages from him.

Hi, this is Max's son, Daniel, in Nova Scotia. We're trying to reach Dad. Michael is here with me. He arrived the day before the attack. Tell Dad he's okay if you can you get a message to him. He must be worried sick. We tried to call. No response. We hear your area wasn't hit. Thank you. Dan.

Jean's eyes flew to the tarp, rolled, and tucked near some equipment that once pulled in fishing gear. She hit reply on messenger then paused. How could she tell them that their father had died? Facebook was such that they would know she'd seen the message.

Send me your phone number, she responded. The number was sent immediately.

She called and in a broken voice told them the news, eyes taking in the scene before her as they slid forward towards a dock.

"Thank you for trying to save my dad, to bring him to safety, we'll be in touch about arrangements," Dan said.

Jean sobbed, and whispered goodbye. She wiped her eyes, her tears stinging her face. She inhaled and hit the app to end the call. She saw the app next to it and tapped it on impulse. Her bank opened to its log-in page, and she pressed her thumb to it. And there it was. Her bank balance. Enough to live on for the rest of her life back home on Desolate Island, enough to get her a good start in a place like Sept Iles too, if it was worth anything now.

Things were oddly normal, as though the events of the world hadn't had any impact. Traffic moved, the driverless cars sharing space with the other vehicles. Even the quiet of electric autos seemed noisy to her. People walked, looking at devices instead of each other, and at dusk the streetlights would come on as though electricity were magic not a luxury.

Once docked, a RCMP officer came aboard.

"I'm Constable Beaudreau. I'll need to talk to you before you can leave the boat," he said, reaching out to shake her hand, uncomfortable with this role but since The Emergency Measures Act had been ordered by Prime

Minister Latimer, he spent a lot of time doing things that he'd never done before.

"I'll need identification from all passengers and crew before I can let you off the vessel."

"Yes, we have all of that," Mallory said. She retrieved the waterproof pouch that held the passports, driver's licenses, birth certificate and so on of every passenger. Except Adam. The officer listened to their story of how Max had died and how they had rescued the young American.

"I'm going to need you all to stay on board," he said, after matching each to their identifying papers. His friendly demeanor chilled as he eyed Adam. He handed the bag back.

"He's just a sailor," Jean offered, worried. But Boudreau stalked away and spoke to his partner who moved their car closer. A short while later he returned, this time accompanied by two military officers.

Jean took them into the galley. The enclosure barely had room for those who came with them and was claustrophobic with the two military police and the Mountie in their space. Everybody laid in bunks or sat on the benches. RJ and the other men, free to leave, had gone to town to check things out.

"The Canadians are good but this guy's an American. He has no ID and so I wasn't sure what to do. We can't just let anybody into the country."

"Thanks, officer. So, Adam, let's talk." The army lieutenant turned to the American who was seated at the galley table. Ashlyn had been playing a card game with him and she moved over to allow the man to sit.

"What happened, young man?" His voice was firm but friendly.

"We were attacked, sir."

"By whom?" he held a pen over a notebook.

"I don't know, sir. I was asleep. I woke to a loud bang, threw on my suit, and went out, we were already sinking then. I jumped into the water and made my way as far from the ship as I could. I found something floating, climbed onto it and waited. I was there for hours. The boat caught on fire, the water was on fire, it had died down a lot when I got picked up."

"You are a very lucky man. Were there no other survivors?"

"No, not that we saw, sir. We all scoured the water as we came through. Everybody was dead, hypothermia. We didn't have time or space to pick up the bodies, we needed to get ourselves to safety," Jean answered then.

"Sir, we can't allow you into the country without papers. We've had a real problem with American refugees." He scribbled down Jean's explanation.

"Refugee? No, I want to go back to the US. My papers were on my ship, sir." He looked confused, where could he go?

"You sure you want to do that? It's pretty bad down there."

"Yes, I don't care how bad it is, that's home."

"We heard it was rough in the states, but is it that awful?" Jean moved close to Adam, feeling protective.

"Whatever you heard it's like in the States, it's worse."

"I still want to go back," he insisted.

"Without papers, you might have trouble, but it'll make it easier for us if you do."

"What will you do with him?" Jean asked. She too was confused about where he could go.

"Well if you could get him to an American ship to go home that would be best. You're in Canadian waters now but we've forbidden American ships to come into this port. You see, they're a target and if we let them in then we become one. But there is a US military vessel offshore, if you could get to it, I'm sure they'll take care of you. We might allow a small tender to come get him also. If they were willing to send it."

"Can you set that up? " Jean asked.

"We'll get in touch with the captain. I'm sorry, sir. When the war started all these new immigration regulations were added. We have a lot of people coming to Canada from the US, well from all over, but a lot of Americans. So, they've had to clamp down. In many places we would take you and put you in a detainment centre but there isn't one here, plus you don't want to declare asylum anyway and, well, getting you to one would require breaking our own policies because we, as well as the RCMP, can't be involved in immigration stuff anyway. Crazy, I know."

"I have a question, officer. About something different," Jean said.

"Sure. If I can help."

"Is money still worth the same since the war?"

"There's some crazy gouging in places but here it's not too bad. Do you have money to get by? There are food shortages, so you'll find the prices high on a lot of items."

"They still take plastic or cash only?"

"Still electronic most places. But to be honest, I pulled a pile of cash out, and never leave my pay in the bank. I don't trust the systems you know. After that virus took out those American electrical grids, I think a lot of people did the same."

"Wow. That's terrifying. And thanks. We had no communication. So, I wasn't sure. And yeah, the systems were useless to us after we were hit."

"If that'll be all, I'll be off and try to make arrangements for this young fellow." He turned his serious face back on as he climbed the steps out of the galley.

"Don't worry, Adam, we'll get you home," he said.

"Thanks." The young American smiled for the first time since his ordeal.

"Play Snap again?" Ashlyn asked, and he agreed.

Jean looked around. Everybody appeared gaunt and old, their faces thin and eye sockets hollow. Several months of rations made a negative difference in their health. More than that, the stress of it all had drained the essence out of everybody. And whether they showed active sickness or not, all had been exposed to the poisoned air.

Jean still had waves of nausea. She'd google radiation sickness later. God, she could Google. How exciting was that? She was sure, now that she was out of it, if that's what her problem was, she would survive. She'd already made it further than most. She still hadn't told everybody what had happened to the other boats from the Island.

This handful of people, their hearts broken, their bodies weak, were all that remained of a thriving fishing community, its final residents dying a slow death, while the others who had fled were all lost at sea.

She would ask Roy to help her tell them about the fate of the others, then host a prayer service. Meanwhile she needed to find places for these people to live.

CHAPTER TWENTY-SEVEN

Roy clambered into the galley and Jean looked up from the checker game she was playing with Ashlyn who had learned the game at a remarkable speed after watching her and RJ play. Ralph Sr. was in the bunk and Mallory had gone off to purchase a few items.

"They all got away, okay?"

"Safe and sound, though the Max family barely made the bus. We walked in as it was loading."

Both the Maxes and the Ralphs were gone. Colin and his family, The Ralphs, had taken the bus to Southwestern Ontario, to a tiny town called Grand Bend on Lake Huron, and Marilyn, Dave, and Matt had purchased a small car and were driving to Manitoba where they had family. RJ had cooked a big breakfast for them as a farewell gesture. It had been a tearful good-bye. They would keep in touch, they all swore, but nobody was sure they would. The families were somewhat in shock still about the rest of the town's fate. Left behind in the small boat at the dock were Jean, RJ, Ashlyn, Mallory, Roy, Ralph Sr., and the American man Adam.

Adam Bayfield was a lovely man, with a gentle voice and calm temperament. He never complained about being stuck inside the boat, but it had to be hard on him.

"Any word on my case?" he asked Roy.

"Nothing. The lawyer said that you're better off making it to the American ship somehow, so we're trying to contact one offshore but still no answer. Don't worry, we'll figure it out."

"I'm sorry, Adam. This is so unfair. I can't believe we can't even take you to the border," Jean said.

"Maine is in disarray so I don't think he should go there anyway." Roy shook his head, trying not to think of all the destruction.

"Even if it wasn't, it's not safe traveling through Canada either. Things are crazy. Americans are coming over the border in droves and there are a huge number of Canadians who feel they're dangerous and are trying to have them expelled. The police aren't much help given there are no citizens' rights at the moment, with the emergencies act in place. It might look the same, here in lovely Sept Illes, but this is not the same Canada that we're used to."

"I know the Prime Minister is a jerk and not helping the situation, but these are the *Americans*. They're protecting us from the Russians and the Chinese," Jean said.

"Yeah, in a war *they* started. Sorry Adam, but it's the truth," RJ said. He felt bad when the Americans were bad mouthed in front of Adam, but the truth was the truth. The poor guy couldn't help the actions of his country.

Jean glanced up at the man, who was a lot more than a complication. He had become a liability. They had even been warned by the military police to keep his presence a secret because of a group of people who called themselves The NQ or Nettoyants du Québec, the Quebec Cleansers, a spinoff of the NC, which was a national purity organization, a fringe group that had been spurred on by current government and who held angry anti-American sentiment.

There was a resistance to this by people who knew that regular Americans weren't responsible for the actions of their government but the thousands who had poured over the border at the start of the conflict and swarmed into the cities and towns had angered a certain segment of society who felt the Americans were a threat and might take over Canada. A few who felt this way had taken it to extremes and in some larger centres Americans had been threatened and even beaten. Nothing like that had happened in Sept Illes, but there was an active chapter of NQ here.

"I am sorry," Adam said. "I'm such a problem for you guys."

"Not to worry, we'll work it out," RJ said.

"But what do we do?" Jean asked.

"We wait," Mallory said

"I'm not good at waiting, Mallory. I need to fix things. And this is ridiculous. What has happened to this country? Let's go, RJ. I need to get out of here and figure something out," Jean said.

"Okay, let's do it. Adam, we're going to brainstorm a way to get you home. Meanwhile everybody relax. Jean is on the job!" He winked but RJ too found the situation untenable. He wanted to take Adam out to the US ship but with Max's warning about getting to Quebec and not going back out to sea, it felt wrong. If he did decide to do that it would be with an empty longliner. It was silly and superstitious, but he couldn't risk the others. How could people be hateful towards a group of ordinary folks because they were on one side or another of the war? There were people of Chinese and Russian descent having some trouble too, but the bulk of the anger was at the Americans who were perceived by many to have brought the war out of the faraway lands, to North American. It was all fine when the people being threatened and harmed were strangers but not so much when it came near to their own shores. It was a predictable, human response. But that didn't help Adam, RJ thought as he took Jean's hand and helped her onto the wharf. Not even one little bit.

CHAPTER TWENTY-EIGHT

"So, you have a plan?" she asked when they were away from the others.

"God no," RJ replied. "I just need to get away." The air was warm, spring already well underway. Daffodils sprouted along the edges of buildings and the sun shone high in the sky. Overhead tiny carbon-eater drones buzzed about, cleaning the air.

"The truck and trailer are ready for pick up, so we could go anytime but we can't leave Adam behind alone. I simply can't do that," Jean said

"Me either. I also can't believe how quiet the cars are here."

"Electric yeah, and all the roofs, well nearly all of them have those solar shingles. And the wind poles are kind of cool too."

"We were so far behind," RJ said. The collapse of Muskrat Falls, the decisions by the government that refused to put in the infrastructure for the new electric vehicles because they had to show they believed in the offshore oil even though the situation in Alberta should have shown them that oil was on its way out. Oh, sure, unlike Alberta, they could still refine it to the low sulphur levels the world-wide oil regulations required, and they still had markets, but competition was steep. Then the new artificial Cleanfuel became popular and royalties took a nosedive. The complete shutdown of the oil sand had been buffered somewhat by a swing towards the clean energy industry and the technology required to build it. But oil was still used. The war had led to an uptick in production for Newfoundland long after Alberta's industry collapsed. In fact, that might have contributed to the reason the province was attacked. It was a free-for-all off the coast, the oil fields an abandoned treasure waiting for pirates. Sure, Canada owned it technically but if the Russians or the Chinese or the Americans wanted it, Canada was helpless to stop them.

A long-time visionary government had moved Alberta through the transition in more recent years and now the province supplied the other provinces and territories, and much of the world, with low carbon footprint energy infrastructure that was visible on every continent. The transition had taken a nearly two decades, but a progressive new political party had moved them forward with haste.

Even with the offshore, an inept and corrupt Newfoundland government had led the province into a debt from which they could never return. Bankruptcy led to the loss of all investment in communities and had contributed to the outmigration of over half of the population over the same two decades. If it wasn't for an agreement between the Federal government, who absorbed the island's debt and now controlled it as a territory with a local elected group of managers who had little power, nobody would live on Newfoundland Island at all. Labrador, now called Labrador Land, had severed from the province and joined Quebec back then too. It felt like all that happened a hundred years ago, though it was only twenty.

"RJ—have you checked on things back home? The news—"

"I haven't. Do you want to?"

"I think I need to. But not around people."

"On your A-Tab?"

"It's in my bag fully charged."

"There is a bench over there. I think we should see what it says. Face up to it and get it over."

"I'm terrified to look." Her eyes filled. They had not mentioned the disaster since they left it behind.

"I am too, my love, but I think we need to."

They made their way to a bench, under a cherry tree whose buds had opened as though defiant in the wake of the disaster the earth had faced. The blossoms overhead shaded them. As she fiddled in her bag and pulled out her A-Tab, the voices around them were lyrical, the French familiar. The people milled about in a town virtually untouched by the horrors that were taking place off their shores and around the world. It was surreal.

"Cast projection," Jean ordered the device and a screen appeared in front of them. She pressed her thumb against the air where an image hovered, and it flashed on. She gave it a voice command, shaky as she said the words that would bring images of their home province alive. She stretched out the corners of the screen until it was bigger and more visible, and she moved it so that it was in the darker shady area.

She held her breath as images popped up. A gasp from RJ caused her to reach out and hold his hand.

"Video." Jean trembled, and tears flowed. People walked past, saw her distress, and walked faster.

Drone images showed the scars of destruction that ran for great distances. One video had the drone going for fifteen minutes starting outside the narrows of St. John's and finding nothing that could be distinguished as buildings in the city as smoke rose from the crater. The only sign it had ever been there were a dozen colourful ships that bounced around the harbour, untethered and unmanned at the mercy of the ocean. It was an early video. Later images showed people entering in Hazmat suits, scraping through the debris, finding nothing but charcoal. They also found images of Gander which had been destroyed as well, the American airbase that had attracted the attack decimated under the weight of whatever had been dropped on it. Images of charred bodies, unidentifiable, stacked like fish on a flake filled RJ and Jean with horror and they wept as they scrolled through the photos.

Almost worse than the destruction were the survivors whose eyes were lifeless as the media pressed microphones in their faces and requested they tell their sad stories. So, there *was* media, their news stories just didn't make it to Desolate Island.

Hospital infrastructure destroyed, the sick died of radiation poisoning at their homes in large numbers and the doctors who braved the contamination to help found most people too far gone to assist.

Then they came across the good stories. The heroism in the middle of the horror. People who saved others, who helped evacuate folks to the south coast, were interviewed. The opening of St. Pierre and Miquelon as a refuge for those who wanted to come and recover, France being a staunch Canadian ally. The city of Corner Brook, undamaged on the west coast, opened its homes and hearts to those who wandered, shocked into their city though the ash had fallen on them too, and sickness spread as they tried to survive. Lines of people walked westward to-

wards that oasis, eyes haunted like they'd survived Armageddon, what they'd witnessed worse than dying.

"Close," Jean demanded.

"I'm glad I know." RJ shaded his eyes against the sun-
light.

"I'm not." Jean's face was awash with tears.

"I am. I kept thinking perhaps we should have stayed
to help. I was halfway across and had this feeling that
we were abandoning our place, our people at their worst
time. But now I'm seeing that there isn't anything to help.
Oh, they're trying to be helpful but it's hopeless. And I'm
glad I know this."

"You don't think anybody will be left when all is said
and done?" she asked.

"Oh, I'm sure there will be somebody, some people,
but think of the damage to the survivors, think of what's
left? We did the right thing."

"So many people we know have died." She wiped her
hands to staunch the flow of her tears, but they were end-
less, and it was futile.

"I think every person I know in the province has died,
Jean. Except for those of us who are here."

"What is this? Why? I don't understand." Jean collapsed against him, the horror, the loss. It was a reality
she'd been able to ignore by simply not looking at it. Now
it consumed her.

"It's war. It was all so abstract when it was over there,
away from us. Now we know. But we need to move on,
find a safe place. People do survive and cope and we're
going to. But nothing will ever be the same. I used to think
I had all the time in the world. You feel that sitting on the
island while time passes you by. Half the time we didn't
have the signal to run the air screen unless you worked for

A-Zon, it was so isolated, and it felt so safe. And I was fine with that. God, I loved my life there. But it's over. We're going to have to heal from this whole thing and Ashlyn is certainly going to get a good shot at doing that. But first we have to solve the problem of Adam and I think I know what we're going to do."

CHAPTER TWENTY-NINE

"Are you sure about this?" Adam's eyes were filled with tears as he took in what Jean and RJ—well RJ specifically but Jean because it was her gift too, offered.

"Yes, we've got enough. If you can operate the boat, she's yours. We are going to pack up the truck and trailer and head out to, well, we're not even sure yet, but probably to Northern Quebec or Ontario. We're going to pick a place on the map. We intended to sell the boat but that will just hold us back. Roy, Mallory, and Dad are going with us."

"I can operate her. I am not sure about docking her alone."

"Maybe you won't have to dock. I'm sure they'll come to you when you get close enough. Especially if you raise that US flag before you approach." He nodded to the star-spangled banner in a plastic bag a drone delivery had dropped off on their deck earlier. He didn't tell Adam that he'd learned most of the people who purchased these in Canada were buying them to either paint hate symbols on them or burn during anti-American marches.

"When will you leave?"

"In a couple days. The van works great, the trailer is packed. Everything we need is in her. Jean thinks we should all see a doctor before we hit the road, but we can stay in the RV."

"Okay, so you can give a bit more information on how to run this boat, if she has quirks or whatever. Are there special things I should know about her? Are you sure about this?"

"Adam, we want you to be safe. You're not to blame for this. You are only a regular guy. I'm sorry people have become so hateful. This boat is named for my mother, and she would want you to have it, right, Dad?"

Adam looked around at the galley, his eyes darting from Jean to RJ then back to Ralph who nodded.

"I don't deserve this." Adam's voice broke.

"Of course, you do."

"No. I don't. I really don't." He couldn't say the words, but the shame of past biases welled up in him. He had never been particularly open to others, had never stuck up when things were bad for them, so now, the Canadians treating him this way was nothing he deserved. He would do better. He'd be like Jean and RJ when he got back to Wisconsin. Jean had allowed him to contact his family through A-Tab and they awaited his return. And the first thing he would do is give them a lecture on their own wrong-minded opinions on the people who had come to their country from other places.

"This is very kind." Adam's voice broke, he wiped his hand across his face and shook his head.

The door opened, and Mallory and Roy came in with Ashlyn, her ice cream half gone. The child who had asked if there was ice cream in war, now got one every day to make up for all she'd missed out on. She spoke of her mommy often but had also taken to calling Jean Mama which made her heart bigger each time she did, like that old Grinch movie from forty years back. She had also turned four years old several days prior and was proud to celebrate with cupcakes and a song that night after pizza for supper.

They settled in the galley, and RJ pulled out the guitar and strummed, a habit that had become part of their evenings onboard. There was a gentle roll on the ocean and the boat lifted and dropped. It knocked against the dock and bounced back in a rhythm that consoled them as they listened to the music he pulled from its strings. Turned out Roy's voice wasn't just for preaching and he was about to start in on an old song, the lyrics moving forward from his mouth when a loud shout came from outside and Ashlyn jumped, running into Jean's arms.

"Go to Mallory, sweetie, Mama and I will go see what's going on, okay?" RJ said.

The child reached her hand out to Mallory. The guitar was returned to its spot and Jean and RJ headed up to check on the ruckus. Shouts met them as they opened the wheelhouse door and stepped onto the deck.

"We want the American!" a voice shouted from the crowd of about twenty people who stood on the wharf.

"You have an American on board?" another, a woman, shouted.

"We are from Newfoundland Isle," RJ answered, not answering the question.

"We heard you're harbouring an American and he needs to be handed over to the police."

"Screw the police," a voice roared from the back. "Give him to us. Give us the terrorist."

The boat rumbled under their feet and Jean jumped. Roy came out to the deck. The grinding engine had been stoked to life. Sensing this would anger the riled crowd,

Jean moved towards the painter that tethered the boat to the dock at the stern. RJ caught the movement in his eye and moved toward the bow, shouting to the people, his goal to take attention off Jean.

"Look, we understand your anger at the Americans."

"What, you're not angry? They bombed the shit out of your island!"

"It was the Russians."

"Nobody knows that for sure. We have a theory it was the Americans, so they could have an excuse to bomb Russia."

"You don't know any of that." He wanted to argue with them. It didn't make sense that the Americans bomb their own base in Gander or, more recently, drop bio-bombs on Stephenville and Deer Lake, the only remaining airfields in the place but these guys were caught up in the anti-American sentiment and there was no way he could convince them in time to prevent what was about to unfold.

"We're coming aboard for the Yank," a heavyset man who appeared to lead the crowd, shouted.

"No, you'll not board our boat." RJ wanted to see how Jean was doing with the rope but dared not direct his eyes to her.

"I'm calling the police," Jean said, phone in hand coming up beside him. The boat bobbed a foot off the dock. RJ needed to keep the crowd from noticing.

"The cops won't do nothing, emergency act you know! They will side with us." His French accent was thick, but RJ understood every word.

"They have been in this boat, checked all our papers and we've been approved. Go ask them."

"We did, they said you have an American."

Shit. Of course. How else would they know Adam was aboard? Jean dropped the phone. She reached for a gaff, holding the stick out in front of her.

"Do not come on this boat or I'll stick you with this." she shouted.

"Jean, stop." RJ yelled.

"No, this is bullshit. Get the hell away from our boat!" She took the gaff and pushed it against the dock. The *June Delight* moved away the length of the gaff and kept going, her bow tethered still at the stem. RJ ran in that direction, reaching for the knife he always carried, popped it open, and sliced the rope clear through with one motion.

Plop, a man landed beside him, and another followed. Jean rushed to the bow as the engine revved into reverse and a glance in the window of the wheelhouse showed Adam at the wheel, Roy next to him.

The man, his plaid shirt flapping about a fat belly, pushed at RJ who turned the knife on him. The other man attempted to rush RJ but was slammed by Jean. He whipped his left arm around and knocked her backwards, the gaff flying from her hand, as though she were a mere cat for the kicking.

RJ lifted his right foot and kicked the man who stumbled backwards. Jean recovered and went forward again. She pushed the same man, now off balance, towards the edge of the boat. RJ held the knife in front of him, keeping the fat man at bay.

The second man stumbled backwards but didn't fall so Jean went towards him again. He shifted to one side and Jean flew past him, the wall she expected to strike no longer there. She skidded towards the edge of the boat.

She noted the air under her legs as they slid over the side, and she grabbed for the railing. Suddenly there was a loud splash and then, before she could absorb what was happening, she was dragged on the deck. Another splash and a howl followed the first.

"RJ," she whimpered, the wind knocked out of her preventing the scream she intended.

"I'm here, you okay?"

The boat revved and the air around her picked up velocity as it moved off from the pier.

"I'm fine, close call. What happened?"

"Mal knocked them both overboard, like friggin' Wonder Woman!" RJ raised his hand.

"Just reacted," Mallory met his hand in a high five.

"Good reacting, I say. Wow, well done! You saved my wife, and perhaps all of us. Thank you."

"What was that all about anyway?" she asked as she helped Jean up and they made their way to the cabin.

"They hate Americans. They hate Russians and Chinese too, but Americans are nearby and moving in, so they particularly hate them. The police let them know Adam was here. They probably set it up. Who knows? They are pretending to enforce order but seems they're enforcing anarchy. What a mess." RJ swiped a hand through his hair.

"Okay, so what do we do? Where do we go?"

"We get rid of me," Adam said. "Then you guys go home. Put me in the lifeboat and I'll figure it out."

"No," RJ said. "We'll take you out to the American ship. Instead of you going out alone, looks like we'll have to take you now. Look, it's dark. We can start radioing ahead, trying to figure out their frequency. I think putting you in the life raft is a good idea but not until we're close to them."

"But what if they decide to blow us up?" Mallory

asked.

"Let's hope we can get through to them before they do. We'll approach in the daytime. We will fly their flag and then hand it over to Adam once we set him out there.

"Do we go now? How long to get to her? Do we know where she is?" Jean asked.

"I can find her," RJ said. His eyes narrowed. Max had said never go to sea again, but it was only an hour or more back outside the bay. It would be fine.

"Where is Ashlyn?"

"Downstairs playing."

"Let's all get life jackets on. Just in case," Jean said.

"Put the animals in their carriers."

"Alright. Let's get this underway."

They set about preparing. It was a risk. After what happened to the others from back home and the mess they'd sailed through when they picked up Adam, leaving the security of the harbour had not been in their plans.

"I'm sorry for the trouble I've caused, I should have gone with them. Mallory ordered me to start the engines and so I did," Adam said. He had been quiet as they talked.

"Don't talk nonsense. We'll get you out to your crowd and then we'll head back, grab the RV, and leave in the middle of the night. I think if we're careful, we can get this all taken care of. You'll be safe and we'll be on the road. If we could only make radio contact, that would help. Maybe they can hear us but aren't replying for some reason," Jean said.

As they headed away from the shore and the twinkling lights of the town it was difficult to reconcile the actions of the people on the dock with those encountered as they went about their business. The soft French tones, reassured, offered sympathy for the tragedy they had endured. It bore no resemblance to the horde of hate that had come to the wharf for Adam.

Jean pondered that. Her heart was heavy that such vitriol could exist. She thought of Ashlyn, so sweet and gentle, her fear greatest for her. The rest of them were expendable, worn, but the child, she was the hope, the future, the promise that human beings would somehow survive this crazy time. She wanted to live herself but mostly, so she could ensure that Ashlyn did.

This is what being a mother feels like, she thought as she made her way down into the galley and to the bunk where Ashlyn cuddled a stuffed dog and flipped through a picture book.

"We're going for a ride, Mama?" she asked.

"Yes, we're taking Adam home."

"That's good. Adam is nice. His mama will be happy to have him with her."

"Yes, she will, just like I'm happy to have you with me. Let's get some sleep now, munchkin."

"Promise you'll wake me up to say goodbye."

"If there is time," she said, unable to promise anything anymore in this crazy messed-up world. Not even time to say goodbye.

CHAPTER THIRTY

Jean made her way up to the wheelhouse. She held the steaming coffee out to RJ who leaned in for a kiss before taking it and sipping on its contents. She felt awkward in the lifejacket, but she had insisted they all wear it as a precaution like they had on the trip across the gulf. Well, those who didn't have survival suits. Ralph wore his, but RJ had sacrificed his to Adam given he'd be in a lifeboat alone. He wore a blue PDF instead, which looked nice over his blue plaid shirt.

"At least it's calm this morning." The sun's reflection slanted across from the east as they made their way towards the large ship in the distance. Jean could have enjoyed this trip, she'd always loved being on the water on days like this, the gulls whipping about searching for herring, the sky dotted with fluffy white clouds, the air as fresh as sheets whipped on a summer's clothesline. If she didn't think about it, she could pretend she was home, but RJ himself was a reminder that she wasn't. She hadn't known RJ in peacetime, hadn't been coupled with him until the war drove them together. She was happy for her marriage but would gladly go back in time and give it all up for the peace of a Newfoundland beach, a boil up with friends, and a kayak out to a berg when the currents saw fit to send one her way. Not because she didn't love him but when she thought of all the lives lost, it seemed a worthwhile sacrifice. Plus, you never missed what you never expected to have.

"No luck with the radio." RJ broke through her thoughts. "They may be hearing us but they're not responding. I can hear a Canadian Coastguard ship but they're not answering either. It's so odd, why the two-ways won't work."

"RJ, how close will you go?"

"I don't know. I don't want Adam to be too far that he doesn't get picked up, but I don't want to get noticed. Though, they probably see us anyway with their equipment."

"Not a level playing field, is it?"

"No, it's not. We're sitting ducks. I've never been concerned on the water before. The storms, engine trouble, all sorts of stuff happens when you're out fishing, but that's stuff I know. One time the engine shut off and we had to mayday, and we got towed in and that was nerve wracking but now, there's nothing civil on the water to help in a pinch, everything is navy, and most everybody hostile and paranoid and ready to shoot. Sorry, you know this and I'm only making it worse."

"I was thinking about how we used to cook crab legs on the beach back home. Let's go somewhere with a beach when we leave. A small place in Northern Quebec where we can cook outside, grow things, regain what we've given up in a new place. I don't care if it's salt or fresh water. I want to fish and make food and live until I die with you and Ashlyn, and your dad, Roy, and Mallory. Everyone we have left from home. The cats, the dog."

"I'm in. Let's go as far as the roads take us, then stop.

You can teach me French, teach Ashlyn too. We'll go as soon as we get back. We're nearly all loaded up for the trip. I poked a few more things aboard the truck yesterday. Our identification, the devices. We were so close to leaving, those bastards on the wharf—never mind, it's a delay that's all."

"Think Roy will learn to preach in French?"

"Shhh," he whispered, then added, "So long as he can hear his own voice, he'd preach in pig Latin! Plus, I think Mallory will listen."

Jean laughed, a foreign sound, one she missed. "You noticed that too, uh? I think there is a spark happening there."

"Wouldn't it be nice? I wonder how the Maxes and Ralphs are doing. I'm glad they left when they did. Shit, I think it's moving, grab the wheel."

Jean did as he asked while RJ pulled up the large binoculars and peered through. Still looking, he said, "Yeah, she is moving, turning I think, coming this way. She's closer than I realized now that she's bow towards me. Here, look."

Jean took the binoculars as RJ put hand on the wheel and she lined up the ship through her viewfinder. It was massive, its bow veering around, coming in their direction. She looked at the radar. The blip on the screen gave no indication of reality. The binoculars did.

"This makes me nervous. I think we should send Adam now and turn ourselves around."

"I think you're right. It's his best shot. The lifeboat is almost ready. Go get him."

Jean made her way below, silent as she headed down for Adam. She tapped Roy on the shoulder and Ralph as she passed each of them. They rose without word, eyes towards Mallory and Ashlyn. The three men grabbed coffee from the pot and headed after her. They didn't know what sort of time they had or even what they were doing but coffee would buoy them up and Jean didn't seem to be rushed.

Once they all gathered, RJ directed them to look at the vessel in the distance and they each took a turn peering out and nodding that they needed to do it now.

"We haven't heard from the ship, Adam, but we think the safest thing for all is to put you in the lifeboat with the flag. They won't see you as a threat and likely they'll just pull you up."

He couldn't guarantee that's how it would go but he was hopeful.

"I agree, let's do it. I can make it out there." Adam was terrified, but these people had done enough. He needed to let them get home. Those were his countrymen out there. He'd spotted the symbol of America on the side of the vessel and felt a longing for it. Yes, perhaps his country was guilty of a big part of the destruction happening on the planet but still, they were his people, Americans, who had led the world for so many years as a beacon of hope and democracy. A corrupt government had led them to this mess, but the people were still the same. There were many, probably the majority, who resisted this war from the start. He'd join them when he got home. Having seen the horror of all his shipmates blown to bits in Canadian waters, the friendliest on the planet for most of his lifetime, he now knew the truth. He had scoffed at their opposition to the policies that created this mess, but now he knew them to be right. Perhaps he didn't agree with everything the new government said but he agreed with one thing completely. Peace needed to come to America and the world again and he'd die trying to bring it back, if he ever made it home to Fish Creek, Wisconsin again.

"You get that survival suit situated. You're not zipped up. I'll steam closer yet, but finish getting the lifeboat ready. There are flares in her. Hoist that flag high and we'll lower you down afterwards. It's a calm day. Once you're on the raft, we're going to back away and watch from a good distance in case you need us for a short while."

Jean took the wheel again. Though she was not a seasoned navigator she wasn't useless, and this was easy. Straight ahead until RJ came back. She heard the shuffling on the back deck, but stared forward, eyes fixed on the large grey shadow in the distance. They closed in over the next while, the lines around the ship solidifying as they steamed through the gentle swell of an unfamiliar sea. Jean wished she could keep going, the eastern coast of Newfoundland visible in her mind's eye, a beacon that blinked inside her head, drawing her forward.

But she wasn't going home. Max was gone, his body sent by train to his sons, and the most peaceful place she'd ever known no longer existed, everyone dead or exiled except for a few poor souls rotting in their own beds waiting for death, the town around them full of ghosts and dust.

Ralph Senior's voice vanquished her reverie, landing her back in the middle of a warzone.

"I'm to take the wheel so you can say goodbye," he said in his hushed voice.

Jean walked out as they lowered the inflatable life raft and dropped the ladder. It was far easier than if this were happening in a storm as is often the case with lifeboats. Luck was on their side weather wise. Jean walked to Adam Bayfield and held out her arms, wrapping him in a big hug.

"Remember us," she said. "Please contact me as soon as you are safely aboard."

"I will for sure. Thank you for everything. This boat and all of you saved my life and I feel like I'm leaving a sanctuary. I promise I'll call." He reached out his hand to RJ and thanked him but was pulled into a hug.

"Kiss Ashlyn goodbye for me," he said. "She wanted me to wake her up from her nap, but I told her that it was not likely that I could, so I said goodbye to her last night, but if you can tell her I said it again today… she's a sweetie and, well, I'll miss her." His voice broke and he turned away to the side of the deck, to compose himself, then turned to face them again.

RJ kept the boat steady as the men controlled the raft with ropes. Adam climbed down the ladder, scaling the steps sure-footed as he stepped into the raft with its buoyant sides. His survival suit would have kept him afloat had he not been successful. But he was, sitting back in the bright yellow and orange dinghy with a plop as it rolled under him. He laughed at his lack of steadiness in the small craft.

It was basically a floating tent. It had a roof that could be zipped closed for shelter but was open today to allow him to wave the flag on a pole when he got close to the vessel. The wind was in the direction of the naval ship, so he would meet them as he drifted.

Once settled, they set the ropes free, and the raft bobbed away from them. Jean's thoughts went to the movies she'd seen of astronauts who somehow became untethered from their ships, lost in the depths of space. It had nearly happened to an astronaut in the early thirties, but they'd got him back safe. Hopefully Adam would be saved from floating forever out to sea. He had water and food, just in case. They didn't doubt the ship would see him, but would they bother picking him up?

RJ gave a shout and Ralph geared up the longliner so that they pulled away, leaving him adrift on his tiny vessel on the big wide ocean.

The space between them grew as Ralph moved the ship into a higher gear and soon enough, they were headed in the opposite direction. Adam gave a wave and they returned it. They watched from the stern as the lifeboat disappeared in the distance, until it became a tiny bright spot in a deep blue ocean.

A short while later, they saw a streak of smoke headed into the sky and break into a flash of light. He had set off the emergency flare to attract the ship's attention. They had no way of knowing if this would aid Adam in this journey that they prayed would take him back home to America.

CHAPTER THIRTY-ONE

Ralph and Roy stayed on the deck to look out for trouble. RJ steamed the *June Delight* forward, punching through the slight lop. The wind was at their bow, and she darted up and down over the ripples, the swell less evident with the uptick of the breeze. Jean joined him on the deck after helping Mallory prepare breakfast for Ashlyn. Mallory settled down with her to watch a video.

"Everything good up here?" she asked him.

"All is quiet. I know the waters are supposedly an obstacle course but so far nothing. It is strange to see so little marine traffic."

"Everybody's terrified to be out here. The sky is bright, the sun is up, the water is so calm as it gets out here beyond the bay. There should be fishing boats everywhere, but everybody has abandoned the sea, fearful of what lurks beneath. The attacks have been brutal, so I can't blame them. We'll be safe inside the harbour in an hour."

"We had to do it though and I hope he makes it."

"We did, yes. Adam needed to go home. I didn't mind risking myself, but for the others, and you. I wish I could have left you all onshore."

"Are you afraid?" Jean asked.

"Terrified. I'm counting the minutes until we dock. I never thought I would be afraid of anything out here on the water."

Jean glanced at the clock on the front panel. It was only ten am. They had been steaming for a while, having left the safety of the harbour at dawn, fearing a night trip with lights on would attract attention. She watched a minute go by. Fifty-nine minutes to safety. Then another, fifty-eight minutes.

Harbour. Every single meaning of the word applied. Yes, the inlet on the coast, wrapped by two arms of land was an actual, physical one. There they would find safety from the threats underneath the ocean. That's where they would dock the boat, leave her to whoever wanted her, and take the trailer north to find a new place to call home. But also, they themselves gave safe harbour to Ashlyn and Mallory when they needed it, and Roy too. They'd done so for those who wandered in across the ice in March when the war first made landfall on their shores.

Then there was the other meaning. To keep a thought or feeling, in one's mind. There hadn't been much time to ponder the secret she harboured. She pulled it out now, mulled it over, decided to give voice to it, share it.

"RJ—there is something—"

A great shudder knocked Jean backwards so that her spine hit a shelf sending a shaft of pain through her back. Another rumble had a roll of charts fly loose and one smacked her on the head. She heard screams from a distance as she fell into a great darkness until cold fingers against her skin pulled her from the depths of the black.

"RJ!" she screamed. The frigid digits that tapped at her skin was the ocean, drifting into the *June Delight's* wheelhouse.

She couldn't get her bearings straight. Was the wheel-house in the water? It took a moment to see that she was in part of the boat that had broken off from the impact of whatever had struck them. It was part of the wheelhouse, and it was floating. She flipped over, clinging to the wood, trying to figure out what sort of danger she was in. The wheel was still attached to the piece she floated on. There was no sign of anyone else around. Flames licked up in front of her and she glared at it through her hazy eyes. Where was everybody? She pulled the whistle on the life-jacket and stuffed it in her mouth. Her lips trembled from fear and cold. Water floated in under her with each dip of the debris she floated on.

The whistle's shriek repeated in the cold air. It went unanswered. Jean felt herself weaken and worried she would pass out again. She needed to stay afloat. RJ. Ashlyn. Where was her family? She felt panic well up in her. No, she had to secure herself, then try to find the others. She shook her head, a sharp pain stabbed at her neck, and she groaned.

"RJ?" She tried to scream around the whistle. Nothing. Just the flap of water against wood, the stench of smoke in the air and the flicker of flame a short distance ahead.

Jean tested her legs. They moved. She flexed her arms, then pushed herself forward. The wood dipped in a bit, but the raft seemed stable enough to be able to move. She lifted again, and her body worked. She wasn't that badly injured. She needed to find RJ and Ashlyn. And the others. She was far from shore and there was no marine traffic. She didn't want to die out here, but she wasn't sure how she could increase her chances of surviving.

What if they're all dead? The thought jumped to the front of her brain, delayed by either the blow on the head or shock. Her heart pounded and her belly ached at the possibility.

No, she told herself. I'm alive, they may be too. They are. I just need to find them.

Jean struggled to sit up, but her body was heavy. The raft dipped once more, and she held fast to ridges to keep herself from slipping off it. After some manoeuvring and testing of the stability of what was underneath her, she managed to sit upright on it. The ship's wheel was to her right. It was detached but hanging and she wondered if RJ had been knocked unconscious by the explosion. She couldn't tell where it had hit so she didn't know how the boat had splintered but perhaps he was nearby, floating but unconscious. Perhaps they all were. She called again, from her seated position and blew the whistle between shouts. Until the lights went out again.

Many hours later, she opened her eyes to meet those of a stranger.

"We got you," the man said. "She's coming to," he yelled to somebody else.

"Where am I?" Jean lifted her head and looked around as they fussed over her. She was no longer on the wooden raft. Now she was in some sort of flat red boat.

"We're the coastguard, you're safe."

"The Coastguard? The others. Did you find RJ? Ashlyn? Where is my family?" she screamed.

The two men looked at each other, then looked to the left of where she lay, then back at her. She followed their glance. There they were, red lifejackets in place, arms placed across their chests, Mallory, missing a leg, half her face blown off, and someone else. She lifted further to see who it was as another man moved to put a tarpaulin over them. But not before she saw perfect little four-year- old

Ashlyn, dead on the deck of the Coastguard tender. She let out another scream, this time a primal painful heart-wrenching howl that was drawn from the depths of her broken heart. She screamed and sobbed until she fell into blissful unconsciousness again, her last thought that she wanted to die.

Ashlyn on the deck of the Coast Guard before she collapsed in screams, the long, guttural painful cries wrenching loose that were driven from the depths of her broken heart. She screamed and sobbed, until she fell into a still unconsciousness, more peaceful though than she wanted to be.

CHAPTER THIRTY-TWO

How dare the sun of autumn lay shards of light across the green and gold fields, when Ashlyn lay buried under a grove of trees, nothing left of her but dust. Jean watched the men through the window. Without seeming to be affected by all they'd endured, they'd torn up the land, planted seeds, got excited about corn, praised the darkness of the soil, revelled in the sprouts that popped with ease up through this far richer earth, while Jean grieved for the hard, stubborn soil of her lost home.

She did not love it here in this pretty land. The river that ambled down the back of the deck played a foreign song, its bubbling and tinkling nothing compared to the great roar of the ocean. This place did not haul the roots from the souls of her feet so that she implanted as she had back home. This was not Desolate. But she was.

Word from home had come to them as of late. Three people survived there. The remainder succumbed to the disease and were buried in shallow graves in the local cemetery, the survivors too weak to dig too deep for so many. The three survivors had all been airlifted out by a Canadian search and rescue team, their rescue a major news story.

Memories of Ashlyn's stoicism over Max's death

haunted Jean. How could a child be so strong in the face of the death of so many whom she loved when she herself could barely move. She told herself she had to go forward, be strong, live again to honour those who couldn't. But her heart weighed her down.

RJ tapped her shoulder and she darted out of her reverie.

"I'm going to put a kettle on. You want a drop of tea? Roy will be in shortly."

"Let me get it, RJ." Jean went to get up.

"Jean, it's fine, let me get it."

"I said I'll get it!" she snapped.

"I'm sorry, Jean I'm only trying to —"

"No, I'm sorry. I can't seem to get it together. Jeez, RJ, why can't I shake this off?"

"You've been through so much. It's still really soon."

"You've been through more. You lost your arm, your daughter, and your father as well as Max, yet you're out getting this farm in shape with Roy. You've ordered seeds, planted, re-shingled with solar, installed wind towers, and built a root cellar. I've been sitting here wallowing. I know it's not right, but I can't seem to shake it. The war is over, there seems to be a bit of optimism in the news. We have money, we have this farm. I should be coming around, but I can't."

"We're all different. I need to get out there and occupy myself to get through, you need to work through it in your mind. I'm not sure I won't fall apart one day, but I seem okay if I keep moving. As for the arm, got another one." He waved his right arm around and Jean laughed.

"That's a sound I've missed," RJ said, kissing her cheek. "I miss her too, you know. I miss Dad and Max and Mallory. I miss Desolate. I know how you feel even if

I don't show it the same way."

"It's the broken promises. I failed her, you know?" Jean stifled the sob and worked hard to stop the tears at the back of her eyes from moving forward. She needed one tear-free day.

"You broke no promises. We gave her everything she wanted."

"We promised her life. RJ, even the two cats and the dog survived." Tom slept curled up next to Princess, fat from farm mice and content with freedom.

"They were in crates that floated, Jean. You can't keep a child in a crate. And no, we didn't. We promised to care for her for as long as she lived. We could never promise life, life is not something any of us can promise. She said she didn't want to die at three, she didn't. She died at four. She wanted another summer and she saw one, perhaps not the entire summer but she saw the sunshine, le Soleil as they call it around these parts. She had ice cream again. Remember how she wanted to know if there was ice cream in war? And so, we gave her ice cream every day once we got here in Quebec. She lived a good life, and her death was fast. I know you don't believe in an afterlife, but I feel her here, in these fields, practicing her French, chasing rainbows, running with the butterflies. We gave her joy in her last days. I think if we don't find our own joy in the days we have, then we're letting her down. We had to get Adam away. We were forced into doing it in a way that caused this heartache, but you know we did all we could."

On his worst days, RJ blamed himself. Max had said, don't go back to sea again and he hadn't listened. But today was a good day when he could see he had no choice.

"I know, I don't blame Adam. He blames himself

enough anyway. And I don't blame you. I don't even blame myself. It's useless anyway, what does it change to blame people? I am trying. I really am. I'll make the tea." Jean rose from the chair, feeling RJ's eyes on her back. She needed to shake this. RJ was right. She knew he was. Nobody who loved her wanted her to weep every day of her life. She turned the knob on the range and set the kettle on it. She pulled out the package of bought biscuits and thought, perhaps she should make some. She always loved to bake and this large kitchen with its massive island was a delight. So much room for rolling out the batter.

"Also, the sun rises and the sun sets and hastening to its place it rises there again." Roy burst into the kitchen, Bible verse on his lips. "I know you don't like preachin', Jean, but that's Ecclesiastes and I think we need to keep that as the motto of this new sanctuary we have found here. Because through all our trials and tribulations, the sun is what we could count on. I fed the horses. Jean, you said you used to ride. I think Lady will be perfect for you. I'm a bit scared of them so you're going to have to do what needs to be done to train 'em up. So, RJ, should I give it to her?"

"Give what to me? Something for the horses?" She'd ridden for years in her youth, but mostly horses had been therapy. She'd found two for sale online and they'd checked out. She'd purchased them, hoping that time spent in their company would heal her. They'd arrived yesterday. A lovely paint and a gorgeous percheron. Neither were papered but Jean didn't care. She wanted friends, not pedigrees.

"Yes, give it to her now. Perfect time, Roy. Jean, Roy made you something."

"Oh? What?"

"Let me explain first, okay? We thought we needed to

name this place, figured it should be a tribute to Desolate but that doesn't really suit. I mean Desolate got its name through mispronunciation and time, but it's not a good name if you think about it. We're new here so we figured we would revert to its original meaning. Which is French. So, I made this to put at the side of the road, by the gate."

Roy went to the front porch and RJ held the door open as he brought in what appeared to be a slab of wood. When he turned it around though, Jean gasped, then a swell of emotion lifted inside her and tears burst forth and started down her cheeks. She reached out a hand, tracing the engraved letters.

"*L'île de soleil d'Ashlyn*" and underneath was Est. 2047. At the top, a grove of ash trees adorned it. There was intricate scrolling around the edges and it had to have taken many hours to create.

"Do you like it? We can change it if you don't. I hope I got the Francois right. I asked the lady at the shop, and she wrote it down. Don't you think it's better to call our new place Island of Sun than Desolate? We thought Ashlyn's Island of Sun was perfect. But 'tis up to you."

"I'm not afraid of dying anymore. Are you afraid of dying?" Jean stroked the sign still, off topic. But not.

"No," Roy said.

"I am more afraid of not living," RJ answered.

"If you don't like it—" Roy moved to take it away.

"No, Roy, I love it. *Ile Desolate. Ille de soleil*. I kind of forgot about the sunshine part. Ashlyn will run with the butterflies. We'll make sure of it. We need to make sure she never stops. Thank you both. This is perfect." She swatted at her tears.

The kettle whistled. Jean went to make the tea. The two men looked at each other, unsure if this was a turning point or not. They decided to drink their tea and hope so.

CHAPTER THIRTY-THREE

Three long months without electricity had Jean coming to with a start every time she awakened under the glow of electric lights. The white walls, the bleached sheets, the table on wheels were all too familiar items this past while. She had been fortunate her entire life to not spend one day in the hospital and now she'd seen more of one these past months than she ever hoped to.

"Comment va notre fille?" The perky middle-aged nurse entered the room with a tray of vials. She set it on the table and reached over the tiny bassinet.

"Our girl is quiet as a mouse, so far," Jean replied, her French nearly impeccable again now that she had been speaking it for months as her primary language. Still awestruck by the tiny human she'd delivered a few hours earlier, she smiled. Jean sat up, feeling stronger than she thought she ought to. She tugged at her gown to make sure she was all set, then flipped her legs over the side of the bed.

"That hair! She needs barrettes already." The nurse stared for a moment at the pretty baby.

"Barrettes! I'll put that on the list for next time," Roy said in English as he walked into the room, his limp barely noticeable. He kissed Jean on the forehead and dropped a chocolate bar in her lap.

"You understood what she said? Why don't you an-swer in French? Don't be rude!"

"Oh yes, I understood but my spoken French is *tres* terrible," he said. "I am far more eloquent in English." He turned to the nurse, "You know I used to be a minister back home, preaching on Sundays. Well, a lay minister. Do you speak any English?" he asked.

"*Non*," the nurse lied. She wrote something in the chart before speaking again. "I have to take a blood draw. If that all comes out okay, we'll get you released," she said with a sidelong glance at Roy.

He walked to the bassinet. "Father God, this little mir-acle of ours, she needs your loving hand to touch her, to make her life long and peaceful." Roy waved his hand over the child as though he were performing a magic trick. He glanced at Jean. "You look forward to being home, I bet."

"Yes. I do but—" Tears welled up in her eyes. She longed to take the baby home, hold her, feed her, raise her. Still, her emotions were all over the place. Maybe now that she wasn't pregnant anymore, they would level out.

"I know, I miss her—them, too. We always will. Each new thing is a reminder of what they're missing. Look, I'll be right outside. I'll come back in when the nurse is finished with you."

"Thanks, Roy."

The nurse wrapped a band around her arm, then placed a plastic strip, attached to an A-Tab over her skin. Her veins became visible on screen and the nurse moved it and tapped her where the largest one had shown. Jean stared out the window, oblivious to the prick of the nee-dle. Cars were pulling into the parking lot, visitors stop-ping by to visit loved ones. As the nurse filled the little vials with their multi-coloured caps, her mind slipped back to that day. She might as well let it go back there, she had no control over her thoughts, the trauma leaving her with constant anxiety.

She'd been rescued by the Coastguard, relatively unharmed by the explosion that blew the *June Delight* to bits. Somehow, Jean remained on a floating corner of the wheelhouse when it slivered into pieces.

She looked at her daughter. This beautiful child had survived inside her, despite everything. There was no indication the radiation had affected her either. The little girl, the perfect blend of her mother and father, slept without a care in the world. Her second child. Ashlyn's life had been dashed away by a cruel blow on a dangerous sea by strange men who cared for their power more than the lives of innocent.

The secret that had been on her lips to RJ before the bomb went off was now a reality. Yet there were so few people to call, to share the news with. Her aunt in Toronto had been thrilled and would come visit in a month or so. That was about it. Though the people back on Newfoundland Island were rebuilding, none of them were her people.

From the dust and destruction there seemed to be a surge of resilience in Newfoundland. A motivation that had been missing before the war now resided in the hearts of the survivors. Corner Brook was the centre of the province now and with help from the Federal government, a new wing was being added to the hospital to aid in the healing of those who remained. The power was restored, the old system finally being replaced by new technology that had spread through the rest of the country a decade before. And best of all, the war was over.

"There, you're set," the nurse said, pulling her from her thoughts back to the present. "I'm sure it's all good. You might as well get little *mademoiselle* dressed up for her trip home. And yourself too".

"*Merci*," Jean replied. Had it only been six hours since the birth? It felt as though Abella had been here forever. The novelty of the tiny face had Jean in a bit of a trance.

"Her name is Abella. It means 'breath'," she'd explained to RJ after her birth. "Because we only live from one breath to the next and that is all we can promise her. Abella Ashlyn Adler-Drake."

"We can promise her ice cream," he said.

"We can try," Jean had replied.

She stood, tested her legs, and nodded. Strong, yes. She reached for the baby, lifted her up and out of the bassinette, to sit and nurse before changing her into a going-home outfit.

"Here, let me help!" RJ's voice came from behind a large spray of flowers.

"Hi, okay, you put the flowers down there, on the table and come help me get set up with the cushion.

"She's awake? Oh, her eyes, look at her eyes," RJ gushed, flowers discarded, forgotten, finding the "C" shaped cushion for his wife, settling it on her lap with his one arm, his thoughts only of his daughter and her mother.

"Yeah, they're like mine," she said. The child, a carbon copy of Jean, showed nothing of her father in looks. But RJ was in there, something about her expressions and movements were all him.

Little Abella tucked her head towards Jean's chest, rooting for milk and her parents laughed at her impatience. The baby made a little cry as Jean pulled open her gown.

"She's starved, give her a boob!" Roy said.

"Stop looking at the wife's boobs!" RJ joked, pretending to block the view.

"Seen one you seen them all," Roy countered. "Plus, I'm a man of the cloth, above such things."

"Sure, and you weren't out there flirting with that nurse. No, not at all."

"I was caring for her immortal soul," Roy cracked. A big grin spread across his face. He'd become close to Mallory before she died and watching his two friends had awakened in him a desire to find somebody to share life with. He hadn't given much thought to it before, but now, he would look. Maybe he'd even have a family. Second chances put ideas in men's heads and Roy, a confirmed bachelor from a young age, now thought perhaps some companionship would be a good thing. He had work in town and on the farm and had plans to build a nice house beside Jean and RJ's place. Now he just needed to meet the right person.

"So, we're released as soon as the bloodwork comes back. Then we can go home," Jean said.

"Excellent news. You're sure you're ready?"

"Yes, I'm feeling really good. Have you told Adam about the baby?"

"Yes. He sends his congratulations. There'll be a gift from Wisconsin coming in the next few weeks. Sent off messages to the Maxes and the Ralphs too, all send their love." His voice broke a bit when he said his father's name.

Ralph Drake Sr. had been located by the Coastguard before any of the others, dead in the water. RJ had been found not far from him, near death, left arm not much

more than ground meat. Quick thinking by the Coastguard and an amputation saved his life. Roy floated in his
survival suit, blown clear of the wreckage and completely
uninjured except for his hip. He still had a wobble in his
walk, but it should go away in time. Mallory and Ashlyn had died from the impact of the explosion which appeared to have hit the galley dead on. While Ashlyn had
appeared unwounded to Jean, her entire back was blown
off by the impact. Jean's one good fortune that day was
not seeing the extent of the trauma that the child's tiny
body sustained.

Tears welled up in Jean's eyes. She wiped them away,
looked back down at Abella, and spoke.

"You would think being in a warzone would toughen
you up. But I'm weaker and sobbier than I've ever been.
Does that make sense? Isn't it time I get over it all?"

"It makes sense to me," Roy responded. "I'm a mess,
truth be known. I'll never venture out on a boat again as
long as I live probably. And I wasn't carrying a baby for
all these months to muck things up."

"It's because we can't pretend anymore. We can never
console ourselves that it's all happening somewhere else.
We can never hold in the back of our mind that it happens
to *them*. It can happen to anyone. It happened to us, to all
those people we loved. It destroyed our town, and that
reality is what makes us weaker." RJ rubbed Jean's shoulders. They'd held each other through enough pain for several lifetimes and they'd do it for the rest of this one.

"It'll make us stronger in the end though," Roy said.
"Now that we know, we can fortify against it. Our bodies
are weak, disposable, but our souls are immortal, forever.
If we look to the Lord, he can lead us forward. Yea though
I walk through the valley of the shadow of Death—I'm

doing it again aren't I? Preachin'?" Roy stopped.

"You're doing it again, yep," RJ said, a grin on his face.

"I kind of like it." Jean's face broke into a smile. There was something warm and comforting about Roy's impromptu sermons. Not their content, but rather their familiarity. It reminded her of home.

"Yeah? Okay then. Yea, though I walk through the valley the shadow of death I shall fear—"

"Not that much!" she said, slapping his leg.

Laughter filled the air, a song in the sterile room.

Abella popped off and turned her tiny head towards the adults, her large eyes surveying the people in charge of her world. She absorbed the mirthful noises. She met her mother's eyes and Jean shhh'd her and lifted her to her shoulder for a burp.

"It is good to be born into laughter," Jean said as she patted the baby's back.

"It is," RJ said.

Roy nodded.

The nurse popped her head into the room and in French said, "The midwife says you don't have to wait for labs and signed your papers. You're sprung." She gave a two-thumbs-up.

"Wonderful," Jean said as the baby let out a tiny belch. They fussed over her as if she'd said something profound, laughing at their own doting of this child, the miracle that led them towards a new light.

Soon, RJ and Roy busied themselves with the baby seat, setting it up on the bed and gathering Jean's things for the ride home.

Leaning the infant away from her in her lap, Jean met Abella's large eyes. The child stilled, a look of contentment on her face, tiny lips pursed as she studied her mother, who whispered to her.

"I will give you as many happy summers and ice creams and peace for as long as I can, sweet Abella. Now let's all go home to *L'île de soleil d'Ashlyn*."

And so, they did.

ABOUT THE AUTHOR

Carolyn R. Parsons is a Newfoundland & Labrador author with a background in freelance journalism. She served on the board of the Writers' Alliance of Newfoundland and Labrador for two terms until 2021 and is the author of six published books including *The Forbidden Dreams of Betsy Elliott* released in 2019 and *The Key of Impasto* novella, a Slipstreamers book by Engen Books in 2020.

In 2021 she was chosen as one of 125 authors from around the world to have her entire body of work launched to the moon on the Peregrine Mission via SpaceX and NASA as part of their lunar time capsule Writers on the Moon payload. The launch is scheduled for June 2022.

She married Kent Chaffey in front of 18,000 people in the Zamboni corner during the first intermission at a NHL hockey game in New York City in 2012 and together they have raised four children.

www.ingramcontent.com/pod-product-compliance
Lightning Source LLC
Chambersburg PA
CBHW011647010726
47495CB00011B/2955